The Foreign Soul
and
The Angelus

The Foreign Soul
and
The Angelus

by
Guy de Maupassant

translated and edited by James Wilson

Duchy of Lambeth
41 Elmcourt Road
Lambeth
London SE27 9BX

—
2008

All rights reserved. No part of this publication may be reproduced, stored in a retrieval system, or transmitted, in any form or by any means, without the prior permission in writing of Duchy of Lambeth, or as expressly permitted by law, or under terms agreed with the appropriate reprographics rights organization. Enquiries concerning reproduction outside the scope of the above should be sent to Duchy of Lambeth, at the address below. The author's moral rights have been asserted.

Published by:
Duchy of Lambeth
41 Elmcourt Road
Lambeth
London SE27 9BX

Introduction, Select Bibliography, Chronology, Note to the Text, Translations, Notes, Appendix © 2008 James Wilson
L'Ame étrangère first published in French in 1894 in *La Revue de Paris*
L'Angélus first published in French in 1895 in *La Revue de Paris*

Cover artwork: © James Wilson
Book design: James Wilson

Typeset in the Duchy of Lambeth by the Duke
Printed and bound by Lulu.com

ISBN 978-0-9558525-1-0
British Library Cataloguing-in-Publication Data
A catalogue record for this book is available from the British Library

Acknowledgements

I would like to thank Rick Wilson for his helpful comments and suggestions; Jacques Bienvenu for supplying me with a copy of the article 'Les trois versions de *L'Angélus*', from *L'Angélus*, journal de l'association des amis de Maupassant, enabling me to locate some secondary sources on *The Angelus*; and Stephen McNeilly for his aid in matters of design and typesetting. Thanks also to Thierry Selva and his website <http://maupassant.free.fr> which has the vast majority of Maupassant's texts online in French and some in translation too; and to Noëlle Benhamou and her site <http://www. maupassantiana.fr> which has an excellent bibliography and is the best place to keep up to date with all things Maupassant.

JW, 2008

Introduction *James Wilson*

Guy de Maupassant is rightly famed as one of the greatest exponents of the short story and he was proud of having reinvigorated French interest in the form, 'C'est moi qui ai ramené en France le goût violent du conte et de la nouvelle' ['It's me who has given France its great predilection for the short story and the novella'],[1] but later on in his prolific but tragically short career as a writer, he virtually abandoned short fiction (and journalism) in favour of novels and plays. As Francis Steegmuller points out, 'Between 1882 and 1887, inclusive, he had written almost two hundred and fifty [short stories]; in 1888…he wrote only six…[and] almost no articles at all'.[2] Maupassant's return to writing for the theatre (he had written several plays in the 1870s with *Histoire du vieux temps* being performed at the Troisième Théâtre-Français, Paris, on February 19, 1879) was largely with commercial reasons in mind:

> Il faut donc que j'avise à gagner ma vie sans trop compter sur la librairie et je vais essayer du théâtre que je considère comme un métier, afin d'écrire mes livres absolument à ma guise sans me préoccuper le moins du monde de ce qu'ils deviendront. Si je peux réussir au théâtre je dors tranquille, sans abuser d'ailleurs de ce trafic pseudo-littéraire.

> [I should bear in mind not to count too much on the bookshops for earning my living and, so I can write my books absolutely as I wish without being

worried in the least what becomes of them in the world, I'm going to try the theatre which I think of as a job. If I can succeed in the theatre without overusing that pseudo-literary trade, I'll sleep easy.][3]

If drama could take care of the bills then Maupassant would be free outside of that to write what he wanted in the way he wanted. And it seems that his preferred form was now the novel. He published *Pierre et Jean* in 1888, *Fort comme la mort* in 1889, *Notre cœur* in 1890, and then began work on two further novels, translated here into English for the first time, *The Foreign Soul* [*L'Ame étrangère*] and *The Angelus* [*L'Angélus*]. Both were unfinished when Maupassant died.

When Maupassant made the conscious shift from shorter to longer fiction, his health was worsening and his ability to write was becoming affected, first physically and, later, creatively. He had been infected with syphilis in his youth and was now complaining more and more often of troubles with his eyes, migraines, and feeling cold. He spent increasing amounts of time away from his Paris home in the warmer climes of the Auvergne, the Côte d'Azure and North Africa. His work rate was slowing down (it was nevertheless still impressive), partly because of his ailing health, but also partly of his own volition: 'Je vous ai dit et je répète sans pudeur que je compte produire fort peu, fort lentement, et me vider dans chaque phrase et dans chaque ligne, mais je désire que cet effort concentré me rapporte autant que les menues besognes des journaux.' ['As I have said to you and I unabashedly repeat it, I intend to produce very little very slowly, and to pour myself into each phrase and each line, but I want this concentrated effort to bring me in as much as the trifling newspaper pieces.'][4] It seems that this slower, more deliberated writing process was a return to the principles of his literary master, Gustave Flaubert. Principles that he had recently re-examined in his essay 'Le Roman' ['The Novel'] which prefaced *Pierre et Jean*, and which revolved around a painstakingly careful choice of language:

> Quelle que soit la chose qu'on veut dire, il n'y a qu'un mot pour l'exprimer, qu'un verbe pour l'animer et qu'un adjectif pour la qualifier. Il faut donc chercher, jusqu'à ce qu'on les ait découverts, ce mot, ce verbe et cet adjectif, et ne jamais se contenter de l'à-peu-près, ne

jamais avoir recours à des supercheries, mêmes heureuses, à des clowneries de langage pour éviter la difficulté.

> [Whatever it is that we want to say, there is only one word to express it, only one verb to animate it and only one adjective to qualify it. So we must search for that word, that verb and that adjective until we have found them, and never be contented with a vague approximation, never resort to the trickeries or clowneries of language, however apt, to avoid the difficulty.][5]

And principles that would have been fresh in his mind as he started work on *The Foreign Soul* and *The Angelus* in 1890, for it was in this year that Maupassant was involved in organizing the inauguration of the monument to Flaubert in Rouen, which took place on November 23.

Maupassant's focus on the novel, his reduced literary output and slower, more studied writing process seem to be linked to the increasingly intrusive onset of his illness and an awareness of his mortality:

> The more he suffered the more he felt the idea of death unbearable. The more futile existence was the more difficult it seemed to leave it without doing anything about its futility. He had hitherto resisted the natural temptation of man to try and defeat death by producing masterpieces, begetting children or making common cause with hoped-for supernatural beings. He could resist it no longer. When his mind had become an open wound and he felt like howling and moaning with pain, he at last gave in and started writing for posterity.[6]

It is in such a context that we can place the two unfinished novels *The Foreign Soul* and *The Angelus*; it is why the former was abandoned and progress on the latter was such a struggle. Maupassant needed time and patience to create his masterpiece, but time was one thing he didn't have: ill health and mental instability overtook him, he tried to take his own life on the evening of New Year's Day, 1892, and spent the last eighteen months of his life, insane, in a clinic.

The Foreign Soul and The Angelus

(Readers who would like to avoid learning plot details are advised to forgo reading the rest of the Introduction till after the texts)

The Foreign Soul (and Notre coeur)

In the summer of 1890 Maupassant was staying at the spa town of Aix-les-Bains in Savoy, where he was taking the waters. But it wasn't just for health reasons that Aix appealed to him, the town's picturesque surroundings, pleasant climate and vibrant social scene also had an allure and would provide the setting for Maupassant's next literary project, his novel, *The Foreign Soul*, for which he was doing research as he recuperated.[7] It was the second year that Maupassant had gone to Aix, having previously spent time there in 1888, and he would return again in September 1891.

The hot sulphur springs of Aix have been visited for their therapeutic waters since Roman times, curists across the ages drinking the water and bathing and showering in it to treat ailments as diverse as gout, rheumatism, infertility, skin ailments and paralysis. Aix-les-Bains and its fellow French spas became associated with wealth and privilege, being popular destinations for Europe's aristocracy who could afford to travel, holiday and pay for physicians. By the late nineteenth century, when Maupassant was visiting, Aix was still frequented by Europe's royalty and aristocrats,[8] but the town was now just as much centred on pleasure and leisure as it was on medicinal health benefits. The casinos, theatres, lavish hotels and parks were as important as the hydrotherapy establishments; and dress codes, fashion battles, table manners and conversational skills provided rituals to be adhered to as strictly as the taking of the waters. Meanwhile the middle classes were heading to Aix in increasing numbers, the town becoming a destination for the aspirational, representing upward mobility and the chance to hobnob amongst the crème de la crème of society. It was in this town's vibrant atmosphere, surrounded by scenic mountainous landscapes, that Maupassant planned to set his novel.[9]

Any writer is likely to repeat in their work certain themes, settings, descriptions, even favourite phrases and pieces of vocabulary, and for someone to write as voluminously as Maupassant did, this was even more likely.

Introduction

Repetition in Maupassant's works was increased by his claim of being an 'industriel des lettres' [an 'industrialist of literature'] [10] who only wrote to make money—he would always attempt to maximize the income from his work, firstly by publishing his stories and novels in newspapers and periodicals before later issuing them in book form, and secondly by using newspaper articles as a testing ground for ideas that could then be recycled in his fiction. However, even if we bear these practices in mind when reading *The Foreign Soul*, they don't seem to wholly explain away the amount of parallels it has with his previous novel, *Notre coeur*. [11]

Notre coeur is the story of a love affair in the Parisian demi-monde between André Mariolle, a well-off singleton in his late thirties, and Michèle de Burne, a beautiful twenty-eight-year-old widow and society hostess. Mme de Burne gathers around her an exclusive set of male artists, musicians, sculptors, writers and philosophers who all adore her and have, at one stage or another, fallen in love with her. Mariolle is invited to one of her soirées and soon becomes a regular of her set. He too falls in love with Mme de Burne and meets with her favour—in no small part due to the passionate letters he writes her. We follow their liaison, Maupassant showing us how the anguished passion on the side of Mariolle plays against the seeming indifference of the frank and analytical de Burne. As it becomes clearer and clearer to André that he loves Michèle in a way that isn't reciprocated, he breaks with her and flees to a rural retreat in the village of Montigny-sur-Loing. He fails to get over his heartache, but takes some solace from an affair he begins with a pretty waitress, Élisabeth Ledru, who, at least, loves him. After Mme de Burne visits Mariolle in Montigny, the novel finishes with André agreeing to return to Paris and resume his relationship with Michèle, accepting that she will never be able to give him the passion he yearns for. However, he also decides to take Élisabeth back with him, determined to have both 'celle qu'il aimait et celle dont il était aimé' ['the one that he loved and the one who loved him']. [12]

The Foreign Soul and *Notre coeur* have numerous similarities, their chief male protagonists, Robert Mariolle and André Mariolle, respectively, not only sharing the same surname, but also other characteristics and backgrounds: they are both bachelors in their late thirties, well-off men of leisure living off inheritances, popular and respected in Parisian society, of artistic bents, but generally lacking direction in their lives. Both Robert (with Henriette

Lambel) and André (with Michèle de Burne) are introduced to their lovers through friends who have already been in love with them themselves and they are given, as such, forewarnings of the pain and frustrations to follow. Robert knows that Henriette is liable to cheat on him, as their affair commences whilst she is still the mistress of Robert's friend; meanwhile, as André becomes a regular attendee of Mme de Burne's Thursday evening receptions, he is warned by several characters that all the men there have fallen in love with the hostess, become her servant, but not had their love returned—and that his fate will be no different. Nevertheless Robert and André embark upon their doomed-in-advance love affairs and share the same awareness of and irresistible attraction to the artifice and manipulation present in the affections displayed by their beloveds. Robert is fixated by the deceit latent within Henriette:

> he had become attached to her in a strange and stubborn way, not to the being that he had believed sincere, but to the being which he knew was deceitful. He loved this woman with an irritable love, exciting and jealous, he loved her like we love whores [*filles*] who overexcite our desires when we make them our regular companions because they are public creatures who we feel are always ready to slide into the arms of another.[13]

Meanwhile André is seduced by Mme de Burne's coquetry in spite of his realization that it is aimed not at him, but for the sake of her advancement in fashionable society:

> André la regardait, ébloui, et songeant qu'il serait aussi brutalement barbare de la prendre en ses bras en ce moment que de piétiner un parterre épanoui. Leur corps ainsi n'était plus qu'un prétexte à parures, un objet à orner: ce n'était plus un objet à aimer. Elles ressemblaient à des fleurs, elles ressemblaient à des oiseaux, elles ressemblaient à mille autres choses autant qu'à des femmes. Leurs mères, toutes celles des générations passées, employaient l'art coquet pour aider la beauté, mais elles cherchaient d'abord à plaire par la séduction directe de leur corps, par la puissance naturelle de leur grâce, par l'irrésistible attrait que la forme féminine exerce

sur le coeur des mâles. Aujourd'hui, la coquetterie était tout, l'artifice était devenu le grand moyen et aussi le but, car elles s'en servaient plutôt même afin d'irriter les yeux des rivales et de fouetter stérilement leur jalousie que pour la conquête des hommes.

À qui donc était destinée cette toilette, à lui l'amant, ou à humilier la princesse de Malten?

[André was looking at her, bedazzled, and thinking that it would have been just as brutally barbarous to take her in his arms at that moment as it would be to trample on a flower bed in full bloom. And so their bodies were no more than pretexts to finery, objects to adorn: no longer objects to love. They resembled flowers, they resembled birds, they resembled a thousand other things as much as they did women. Their mothers, those of generations past, employed the coquettish art to embellish beauty, but they were primarily seeking to please through the direct seduction of their bodies, by the natural power of their grace, by the irresistible attraction that the feminine form exercises over male hearts. Today coquetry was everything, artifice had become not only the means but the ends as well, for they were using it more to inflame the eyes of their rivals and to whip up their barren jealousy than for the conquest of men.

And for whom was this outfit intended, for him the lover, or to humiliate the Princess de Malten?] [14]

Robert and André are both aware that their affairs are not entirely fulfilling or satisfactory, that they can never possess the women they love as they desire, yet they both return to their relationships after previously terminating them. They also both take flight after their break-ups, Robert to Aix-les-Bains, André to Montigny-sur-Loing. And as they try and get over their heartaches through travel, they find their strength renewed in the mornings, and their minds distracted during the days, only for melancholy and reflection to creep up on them in the evenings. [15] They also find diversion in other women—the Countess Mosska for Robert, Élisabth Ledru for André.

The Foreign Soul and *Notre coeur* have more in common, however, than the two Mariolles—they share the same general subject matters, settings and themes and closer scrutiny finds the same small details and descriptions being used in both works.

Both novels chart painful love affairs in Parisian high society and, although *The Foreign Soul* is set in Aix-les-Bains, they both unfurl against backdrops of exclusivity and privilege in circles greatly preoccupied with fashion. In *Notre coeur*, we witness Mme de Burne's obsession and joy at being *à la mode*, through her dress and appearance, as already demonstrated in the quotation above, but also through the decoration of her apartment and her attempts to add the latest, in demand, artists to her Thursday evening set. In *The Foreign Soul*, the need to be dressed according to the latest fashion stretches to the men, who are all wearing tuxedos in imitation of the Prince of Wales, whilst the setting, the town of Aix-les-Bains, is itself a fashionable destination, an in-season place to be seen, to be swapped later in the year for Cannes, Monaco or other in vogue destinations.

The Foreign Soul and *Notre coeur* each give us psychological insights into either one (*The Foreign Soul*) or both (*Notre coeur*) of the participants in the affairs they chronicle. And Maupassant takes up as a theme in both works the love games and power struggles in relationships between men and women—the battle of the sexes, or, as Paul Bourget would call it, 'the clash of the races'.[16] In these battles, the men, Robert and André, are aware of being manipulated and manoeuvred by their women, but are powerless to really do anything about it, slaves to their sensual and passionate desires and also to the habits and customs they have grown comfortable with. The women, meanwhile, Henriette Lambel and Michèle de Burne, need to exercise control and once they have enslaved the men through their desire, start to test how far they can push their limits of patience and subservience. Henriette cheats on Robert, steals from him and imposes unwanted burdens on him (dinner with her mother, visiting her sister at boarding school). Michèle, fully aware of the strength of André's love, expends less and less time and energy on him, limiting the physical side of their relationship more and more until, at the end of *Notre coeur*, André submits to the kind of relationship that she, rather than he, wants.

Maupassant lets us see the emotional and psychological tussles through his characters' powers of observation and self-observation. The self-analysis of André, in *Notre coeur*:

Introduction

Son attention, surexcitée, aiguisée par la peur de ce mal qui serait peut-être si difficile à vaincre, se fixa sur lui-même et fouilla son âme, descendit dans son être intime, cherchant à le mieux connaître, à le mieux comprendre, à dévoiler à ses propres yeux le pourquoi de cette inexplicable crise.

Il se disait: «Je n'avais jamais subi d'entraînement. Je ne suis pas un exalté, je ne suis pas un passionné; j'ai plus de jugement que d'instinct, de curiosités que d'appétits, de fantaisie que de persévérance. Je ne suis au fond qu'un jouisseur délicat, intelligent et difficile. J'ai aimé les choses de la vie sans m'y attacher jamais beaucoup, avec des sens d'expert qui savoure et ne se grise point, qui comprend trop pour perdre la tête. Je raisonne tout, et j'analyse d'ordinaire trop bien mes goûts pour les subir aveuglément. C'est même là mon grand défaut, la cause unique de ma faiblesse. Et voilà que cette femme s'est imposée à moi, malgré moi, malgré ma peur et ma connaissance d'elle; et elle me possède comme si elle avait cueilli une à une toutes les aspirations diverses qui étaient en moi. C'est cela peut-être. Je les éparpillais vers des choses inanimées, vers la nature qui me séduit et m'attendrit, vers la musique, qui est une espèce de caresse idéale, vers la pensée qui est la gourmandise de l'esprit, et vers tout ce qui est agréable et beau sur la terre.

«Puis, j'ai rencontré une créature qui a ramassé tous mes désirs un peu hésitants et changeants, et, les tournant vers elle, en a fait de l'amour. Élégante et jolie, elle a plu à mes yeux; fine, intelligente et rusée, elle a plu à mon âme; et elle a plu à mon coeur par un agrément mystérieux de son contact et de sa présence, par une secrète et irrésistible émanation de sa personne qui m'ont conquis comme engourdissent certaines fleurs.

«Elle a tout remplacé pour moi, car je n'aspire plus à rien, je n'ai plus besoin, envie ni souci de rien. [...]»

[His mind, overexcited, sharpened by the fear that this malady would perhaps be extremely difficult to overcome, focused on himself and scoured his soul, plumbing the intimate depths of his being, seeking to better know and understand them, to reveal to his own eyes the reason for this inexplicable crisis.

He said to himself: 'I have never been subject to impulse. I'm not a hothead, I'm not a passionate person; I've more judgment than instinct, more interests than lusts, more imagination than application. Deep down I am only a discerning sensualist, intelligent and particular. I have loved life's things without ever being greatly attached to them, like a connoisseur, savouring, and not getting tipsy, knowing better than to lose his head. I reason everything and, ordinarily, I analyse my tastes all too much to submit to them blindly. That is even my biggest fault, the sole cause of my feebleness. And now this woman has forced herself on me, in spite of myself, in spite of my fear and my knowledge of her; and she possesses me as if she had run away with, one by one, all the various yearnings within me. Perhaps that's it. I squandered them on lifeless things, on nature which charmed and moved me, on music, which is a type of ideal caress, on thought which is a gluttony of the mind, and on everything on earth that is beautiful and agreeable.

'Then I met a creature who gathered up all my slightly hesitant and fickle desires, and, turning them towards her, converted them into love. Elegant and pretty, she pleased my eyes; subtle, intelligent and artful, she pleased my soul; and she pleased my heart by the mysterious compatibility of her touch and presence, through a secret and irresistible emanation of her person which conquered me like certain benumbing flowers.

'She has taken the place of everything for me, for I no longer aspire to anything, I no longer need anything, want or care for anything. ...'] [17]

is similar to Robert's, in *The Foreign Soul*, as he recounts his history with Henriette to his friend, the Count de Lucette:

Posing as a strong, sceptical and corrupt man, who rationalized his passions, giving into them or analysing them, according to the current fashion, he claimed to know himself admirably, and to never ignore the dictates of the motives he followed be they instinctive or intentional.

So he kept a check on himself methodically, believing he was absolutely clear-headed and talked about himself with the petty pride of a very gifted man who is fully aware of his qualities; of course he judged as it pleased him to judge, amplifying, according to his vanity, what he was anxious to show, concealing what he was anxious to hide, seeing big with myopic eyes his favourite flaws and merits alike, for anyone who looks at himself is too close to the subject to perceive clearly.[18]

Whilst Michèle de Burne's calm, rational scrutiny of her feelings is none too distant from Robert's either:

> Elle ne se sentait point à l'âme cette flamme dont tout le monde parle, mais elle s'y sentait pour la première fois une envie sincère d'être pour cet homme quelque chose de plus qu'une amie séduisante. L'aimait-elle? Pour aimer, faut-il qu'un être apparaisse rempli d'exceptionnelles attirances, différent et au-dessus de tous, dans l'auréole que le coeur allume autour de ses préférés, ou suffit-il qu'il vous plaise beaucoup, qu'il vous plaise à ne pouvoir presque plus se passer de lui?
>
> En ce cas, elle l'aimait, ou, du moins, elle était bien près de l'aimer. Après y avoir réfléchi profondément, avec une attention aiguë, elle se répondit enfin: «Oui, je l'aime, mais je manque d'élan: c'est la faute de ma nature.»
>
> [...] Oui, elle avait eu de l'élan vers lui, et elle en avait encore, en ce moment, au fond du coeur. Il lui suffirait d'y céder, peut-être, pour que cela devînt de l'entraînement. Elle résistait trop, elle raisonnait trop, elle combattait trop le charme des gens.

> [She didn't feel in her soul that flame that everyone speaks of, but for the first time she felt a sincere desire to be for this man something more than a charming friend. Did she love him? To love, must someone come to light who fulfils exceptional attractions, who is different and above all others, and who is lit up with the halo that the heart reserves for its favourites, or is it enough for him to please you a great deal, to please you till you almost can't do without him?
>
> In that case, she loved him, or at least, she was close to loving him. After having reflected deeply on it, with a sharp mind, she finally answered herself: 'Yes, I love him, but I lack enthusiasm: it's the fault of my nature.'

The Foreign Soul and The Angelus

… Yes, she had felt enthusiasm for him, and she still felt it then, in the depths of her heart. Perhaps it would be enough to give in to it and it would become impulsive. She resisted too much, she reasoned too much, she fought against people's charm too much.] [19]

In their capacity to step outside of themselves and examine their feelings with a rationality out of place with, and perhaps anathema to, emotion, Robert, André and Michèle are drawn from the same stock. And for all three their calculated reasoning is something of a hindrance, barring the way to true happiness.

The calculating natures and self-awareness of Robert and Michèle (not so much André) perhaps make them seem cold and even devious at times, but in spite of this, and in spite of their moving in social circles riddled in two-faced superficiality and hypocrisy, they are possessed of unexpected (and often well-hid) depths of honesty and frankness, morality and correctness. At the beginning of their liaison, Michèle lets André know exactly where he stands, predicting their affair almost in it entirety:

«En tous cas, je vous préviens que, moi, je suis incapable de m'éprendre vraiment de n'importe qui, que je vous traiterai comme les autres, comme les bien-traités, mais jamais mieux. J'ai horreur des despotes et des jaloux. D'un mari j'ai dû tout supporter; mais d'un ami, d'un simple ami, je ne veux accepter aucune de ces tyrannies d'affection qui sont les calamités des relations cordiales. Vous voyez que je suis gentille comme tout, que je vous parle en camarade, que je ne vous cache rien. Acceptez-vous de faire l'essai loyal que je vous propose? Si ça ne va pas, il sera toujours temps de vous en aller, quelle que soit la gravité de votre cas. Amoureux parti, amoureux guéri.»

['In any case, I'm warning you that, as for me, I am truly incapable of falling in love with anyone, that I will treat you just like the well-treated others, but never better. I loathe despots and jealous men. From a husband I had to put up with everything; but from a friend, a simple friend, I choose not to accept any of these tyrannies of affection which are disastrous for cordial relations. You see that I am being as kind as I always am, that I am speaking to you as a good friend, that I am hiding nothing from you. Do you accept to faithfully try out what I'm proposing to you? If it doesn't work out, there will always be time for you to go away, depending on the seriousness of your case. A lover absented, is a lover mended.] [20]

And whilst she continues to involve herself ever more in the duplicitous, vain and scheming world of the competing Parisian salons, she never wavers from her straightforward honesty with André, protesting that 'je ne puis plier ma nature jusqu'à la rendre semblable à la vôtre. Prenez-moi comme je suis.' ['I can't bend my nature until it's made like yours. Take me as I am.'] [21] In this respect, Michèle has a great deal in common with Robert and his assertion that he possesses a deep-seated honesty:

> As for those who aren't honest [...] I despise them, yes, mon cher, I despise them in the name of a certain honesty that I have but don't make use of openly, or, rather, of which I make use solely to make judgments that I put away in my private files. I despise lots of people in this way, lots of things, lots of ideas which I have the appearance of making my delights, for I am tolerant and conciliatory, good-natured and sometimes abrupt, when it pleases me to be abrupt, through caprice. [22]

In the decadent worlds of *Notre coeur* and *The Foreign Soul*, where fashions die quickly and there is nothing new under the sun, sincerity is a quality hard to come by, crowded out by characters with a propensity to gossip maliciously and whose default settings are of arch knowingness and ennui.

From the little we see of Robert Mariolle in the seven thousand words or so of *The Foreign Soul*, it is almost as if he has been spliced together from bits of Michèle de Burne and André Mariolle (or that Michèle and André have been chopped out of Robert).

The links between *Notre coeur* and *The Foreign Soul* extend to surprisingly small details: In Robert and Michèle, both novels feature characters who collect rare and expensive objets d'art to decorate their homes and show off their refined tastes.[23] The question of blondes dying their hair is brought up in both works.[24] And on another hair-related matter, Maupassant uses similar imagery when describing two dark-haired foreign women. Firstly, in *Notre coeur*, we have a description of the Italian Mme de Bratiane: 'Immobile, pâle sous ses pesants cheveux noirs, qui semblaient avoir été trempés dans de la nuit' ['Motionless, pale beneath her mass of black hair, which seemed as though it had been steeped in the night']. Then, in *The Foreign Soul*, the Romanian, the Countess Mosska, is described as: 'having on her brow and temples that thick eruption of black hairs which seem to encircle a woman with the night.'[25] Both novels feature passing characters named Epilati.[26] In both novels the Mariolles, Robert and André, have their positions in new social circles confirmed by the invitation of their respective hostesses to join them in a tea drinking ceremony.[27] And both novels depict romantic intimacy with scenes in which women read to men.[28]

The reason for this somewhat extended analysis of the similarities between *The Foreign Soul* and *Notre coeur* is that it should be useful in helping to determine when *The Foreign Soul* was composed and what Maupassant's intentions for it were.

In looking at the composition of *The Foreign Soul*, it would seem that there are three hypotheses for its similarities to *Notre coeur*: 1, Maupassant wrote *The Foreign Soul* after *Notre coeur* oblivious to the similarities; 2, Maupassant wrote *The Foreign Soul* after *Notre coeur* fully aware of their similarities; or 3, Maupassant wrote *The Foreign Soul* before *Notre coeur*.

Arguments for the first hypothesis can be split along two lines: either along the grounds of Maupassant's ailing mental health; or, on those of Maupassant the 'industrialist''s commercial indifference.

Without doubt, Maupassant's health was on a downward curve from the late 1870s up until his premature death in 1893. The onset of the syphilis he had contracted in his youth affected him physically—heart palpitations, rheumatism, migraines, hair loss, eye troubles, intestinal problems—and mentally—depression, growing pessimism, megalomania and hallucinations. The difficulties with his eyesight, in particular, affected his ability to write from *Fort comme la mort* onwards.[29] Francis Steegmuller seems to support this notion that Maupassant's declining mental capacities are to blame for *The Foreign Soul*'s similarities to *Notre coeur*: 'The hero, in the fragment that survives, bears the same last name as the hero of *Notre Coeur*—confusions in Maupassant's life and writings now become more numerous.'[30] Were it just a question of the same surname being used, I might agree with Steegmuller, particularly as in the manuscript of *Notre coeur* we can see that Maupassant altered several character names.[31] However, as I hope I have demonstrated, the similarities between the two works stretch far beyond two characters sharing the same last name. Can Maupassant's memory really have been so weak that he finished one novel and started, as his immediate next project, to unwittingly write the same novel over again in a slightly different setting? And yet in a prose so clear and lucid, with an 'exactness of expression' so admired by Paul Bourget?[32] If so, that would explain why Maupassant put aside *The Foreign Soul*, realizing he was just rewriting *Notre coeur*. But his mother's testimony suggests a different reason for suspending work on *The Foreign Soul*:

> He abandoned [*The Foreign Soul*] not through caprice—his mind was too disciplined to waver between two inspirations—but because the heroine was Romanian and he wanted to live in the same environment as her. And he had resolved to accept the invitation of Carmen-Sylva to spend a few weeks at her court.[33]

If he had been unknowingly rewriting an earlier work, a less successful work, maybe I could understand it, but I find it hard to believe that his memory had disintegrated to such an extent that he would do this in two successive projects, especially when *Notre coeur* had been such an autobiographical work.[34] The chronological proximity of the two works, one after the other, is also why I discount Maupassant the 'industrialist' obliviously rewriting the same book.

Most writers have preoccupations with certain themes and ideas to which they return again and again, often unwittingly, in their body of work. Maupassant was no different and, if we bear in mind his desire to maximize the income from his writing, perhaps even more liable than others to issue material with a family resemblance to previous works, unconcerned at similarities so long as commercial success wasn't compromised. But nowhere else in Maupassant's body of work does he unintentionally write works so similar. Intentionally, yes, in his dramatic adaptations of his short stories, and in rewriting, revising and developing earlier stories such as 'Le Horla'.³⁵ But unintentionally, I don't think so, especially not in contiguous pieces.

The second hypothesis is that, in writing *The Foreign Soul*, Maupassant was fully aware of its similarities to its predecessor, *Notre coeur*. Here Maupassant would be writing a companion piece or parallel novel—similar settings, themes and characters, but the Mariolle 'brothers' gravitating in opposite directions in each text. In *Notre coeur*, André Mariolle is growing weary with the high society he inhabits, but he has fallen in love with one of its guiding lights and hostesses, Michèle de Burne. His feelings aren't returned as he would like and he gravitates 'downwards', taking solace in the love of a girl from the lower classes and relaxing away from society in rural seclusion, enjoying nature and the more primal pastimes of walking and fishing. Nevertheless he can't shake Michèle from his system and returns to her and Parisian society in the end. In *The Foreign Soul*, Robert Mariolle gravitates 'upwards', fascinated by and aspiring to enter the elite social circles populated by aristocracy and royalty. He is in love with a girl from the lower classes, Henriette Lambel, a courtesan and a concierge's daughter with whom he has been living in a domesticity increasingly withdrawn from society. Like André, his love isn't returned as he would like, but he takes solace in the lively atmosphere of Aix-les-Bains and its casinos where he falls for the beautiful Romanian, the Countess Mosska. Had Maupassant continued writing, perhaps Robert would have completed the parallel love / class triangle and returned to his unhappy love affair with Henriette after having sojourned at the Romanian court. The overriding bleak conclusion of both stories would be the same no matter what direction taken: that there is imbalance in all loves and passions and an inability to ever truly know someone.

The third hypothesis is that Maupassant wrote *The Foreign Soul* prior to *Notre coeur*, it either being an early draft for, or abandoned for, the latter. This hypothesis hangs largely on a reading of Maupassant's correspondence with Ferdinand Brunetière, editor of *La Revue des Deux Mondes*, the oldest and most influential French literary review and the one that would first publish *Notre coeur*.³⁶

Maupassant once declared a list of 'dishonourable' things that he would never do: 'I will not write for the *Revue des Deux Mondes*. I will not be a member of the

Academy. I will not be decorated. I will not marry.'[37] Maupassant never put himself up for election to the Académie française, he turned down the Légion d'honneur and he never married, however he did break his list of don'ts by writing for *La Revue des Deux Mondes*. Maupassant appears to have come round to the idea in 1887 after receiving a flattering review of *Mont-Oriol* and of his progression as a writer by Brunetière in the *Revue*'s March 1 issue. Maupassant wrote to thank Brunetière[38] and by the end of the year had agreed to write for them:

> J'ai promis à la *Revue des Deux Mondes* une nouvelle; mais je ne sais encore quand vous l'aurez, mon roman n'étant pas fini et n'allant pas vite.
> Le titre de la nouvelle que je vous donnerai est «Les Cœurs étrangers».

> [I promised the *Revue des Deux Mondes* a novella; but I don't yet know when you'll have it as my novel isn't finished and isn't going too quickly.
> The title of the novella that I'm going to give you is 'Les Coeurs étrangers'.][39]

The next mention in Maupassant's correspondence of the work in question for the *Revue des Deux Mondes* is in a letter to his publisher, Victor Havard, a year later:

> Dès que mon roman sera fini, je commencerai une nouvelle pour la *Revue des Deux Mondes*. Je vous la donnerai en tête du volume que je vous ai promis, car je ne sais pas du tout quand je ferai celle dont vous m'avez indiqué le sujet. Si vous voulez annoncer ce volume, qui sera prêt au printemps, en voici le titre:
>
> *Les Cœurs étrangers*

> [As soon as my novel is finished, I'm going to begin a novella for the *Revue des Deux Mondes*. I'll give it to you to head up the volume I promised you, for I don't at all know when I'll do that thing whose subject you

pointed out to me. If you want to announce this volume, which will be ready by spring, here is the title:

Les Cœurs étrangers] [40]

By August this *nouvelle* was developing into something longer: 'Je vous ai promis une nouvelle. Cette nouvelle quand j'en ai arrêté les lignes est devenue un petit roman. Le premier chapitre est même écrit.' ['I promised you a novella. When I reckoned up the lines of this novella it was becoming a little novel. The first chapter is already written.'] [41] And later in the month, as Maupassant gives an approximate timeline for the piece, we find that the title has changed:

> Avant le petit roman que je vous ai promis *L'Ame étrangère* je compte achever une nouvelle que je destinais au *Figaro*. La nature du sujet et l'intérêt que je prends en l'écrivant (?) *(sic)* font que j'aimerais mieux la voir paraître en une ou deux parties plutôt qu'en quinze ou dix-huit tranches. Je ferais pour le *Figaro* autre chose de moins réfléchi, de plus mouvementé, et je vous donnerais d'ici à six semaines ce manuscrit.
>
> [I plan to finish a novella intended for the *Figaro* before the little novel that I promised you, *The Foreign Soul*. The nature of the subject and the interest I take when writing it are such that I would prefer to see it appear in one or two parts rather than in fifteen or eighteen installments. For the *Figaro* I'll be doing something else less thoughtful, more eventful, and I'll give you this manuscript six weeks from now.] [42]

It is then not until three months later that we hear more about the project for the *Revue des Deux Mondes*.

> Vous aurez aussi, dans quelque temps un petit roman que la mort de mon frère a interrompu. Le titre est: *Notre Cœur*. Ce que j'en ai fait me plaît assez. Je me sens dans un courant d'incontestable vérité, et il me porte. Toutes les fois que j'ai eu cette impression le résultat n'a pas été mauvais.

Introduction

> [In a while you'll also have a little novel that the death of my brother interrupted. The title is: *Notre Coeur*. What I have done so far pleases me greatly. I feel that I'm being carried along in a current of incontrovertible truth. The results have never been bad when I've had this impression.]⁴³

From here on in the history of Maupassant's piece for the *Revue* is more straightforward, a definitive title had been settled upon and Maupassant would carry on working on the novel until he finished *Notre coeur* in Paris at the end of April, 1890 and it was published in the *Revue* a couple of weeks later.

The changing of titles from *Coeurs étrangers* to *L'Ame étrangère* to *Notre coeur*, the evolving length of the piece from *nouvelle* to *petit roman*, and the delays, interruptions and misguided estimations for completion become confusing when we are then presented with an unfinished manuscript (*The Foreign Soul*) similar in content and style to the published work (*Notre coeur*), especially when the former apparently bears a draft title of the latter.

The evidence we have from François Tassart and Mme de Maupassant says that Maupassant was researching *The Foreign Soul* in the summer of 1890 and had begun writing it by the autumn before then putting it aside to focus on *The Angelus*.⁴⁴ Yet after looking at Maupassant's correspondence, one could quite reasonably infer that Maupassant started writing *The Foreign Soul* in 1889 for the *Revue des Deux Mondes*:

When he tells Ferdinand Brunetière in August 1889 that the first chapter has already been written, might Maupassant not be referring to *The Foreign Soul*, the surviving manuscript of which consists of little more than one chapter? In his next communication to Brunetière he refers to this manuscript as being entitled *The Foreign Soul*. Then over the next few months a series of distractions affect this project: the transfer of Maupassant's brother, Hervé, to a clinic near Lyons, his subsequent death and funeral, and a change in literary priorities which sees the need to finish a piece for *Le Figaro* ('Le Champ d'oliviers') come first. By the time Maupassant gets back to work on his novel for the *Revue* in November, could he not have decided to tell it in a different way, changing the setting away from Aix-les-Bains and its cast of aristocratic characters—for which perhaps Maupassant would have to do more research to do it justice, the memory of his trips to Aix in 1888 now fading—to the familiar stomping ground of Paris and its literary salons?

The Foreign Soul and The Angelus

There are valid arguments for and against all three of the hypotheses I have outlined for the similarities between *The Foreign Soul* and *Notre coeur*, and any one of them, or combination of the three, could be true. The two main sources about the conception and progress of *The Foreign Soul*—François Tassart's memoirs and Maupassant's correspondence—seem to conflict and so, without further evidence coming to light, we can only make educated conjectures as to when Maupassant was working on this project.

For what it's worth, my guess is that the reason for the parallels lies somewhere between hypotheses two and three. I think that when Maupassant agreed to write something for the *Revue des Deux Mondes* in 1887, he conceived the idea of writing a psychological novel about an unhappy love affair in high society, drawing from some of his personal experiences.[45] He began to work on it in 1889, writing the first chapter of *The Foreign Soul*, but then was waylaid by the death of his brother and by work on other literary projects. When he returned to it he felt that either the setting of Aix-les-Bains or the cast list of aristocratic and royal characters were too far removed from his own experiences to invest the work with the 'truth' that he wanted for it. So he started to write the story in a different, more autobiographical way, resulting in *Notre coeur*. After completing *Notre coeur*, Maupassant decided to return to the earlier version, *The Foreign Soul*, and travelled to Aix, partly to restore his health, but also to refresh his memory and research the setting. He found all he needed in terms of setting and scenery and also managed to get a basis for the character of the Countess Mosska by having his valet, François, follow around a Russian princess.[46] Maupassant resumed work on *The Foreign Soul* and may at this stage have written the 'variant' conversation between Robert Mariolle and the Count de Lucette.[47] He soon realized, however, that he didn't have enough knowledge of courtly life to write about the Countess Mosska as he would like and he decided to put *The Foreign Soul* to one side until he had taken up the invitation of Carmen Sylva and visited her court.[48]

How would Maupassant have developed *The Foreign Soul* had he continued with it? Again we can only conjecture, but it is likely that in chapter two we would have been treated to an account of the Princess de Guerche's expedition to Chambotte, giving Maupassant free rein to describe the beautiful countryside surrounding Aix-les-Bains. After that, who knows? The scant sources we have for Maupassant's plans and work on *The Foreign Soul* all involve foreign female dignitaries;⁴⁹ which, in conjunction with the novel's title, point towards a romance between Robert Mariolle and the Countess Mosska, possibly following it from Aix to Romania later on.

Alas, we are left with plenty of unanswered questions: how would Alexandre Dumas fils' story have been weaved into the plot—perhaps the Countess Mosska would have been somehow imprisoned in Romania against her will? And how would Maupassant have fitted in François' findings on the Russian princess in Aix? What about the violent death or crime that Maupassant asked his valet to keep an eye out for? Would Henriette Lambel have reappeared and won Robert back with her feminine wiles?

Paul Bourget thought *The Foreign Soul* would be 'in the form of a love poem, like *Notre Coeur*, and as a novel of morals, like *Mont-Oriol*'.⁵⁰ With its sharp dialogue benefiting from his recent forays into drama, it could also have been Maupassant's most entertaining society novel since *Bel-Ami* (1885); the seeds being sown for a novel of passion, corruption and ambition, a novel that would be 'perhaps even a little sensational'. ⁵¹

The Angelus

Maupassant began work on *The Angelus* probably in mid to late 1890 and by the end of February 1891 had made it his sole literary concern, putting *The Foreign Soul* to one side for the time being.⁵² He asked his sister-in-law, Marie-Thérèse, to rent him a sunny apartment in Nice for the month of April, where he hoped to finish *The Angelus*,⁵³ however, the physical and mental processes involved in writing were affected by his poor health (in particular his eyesight) and in turn made his health worse:

aussitôt que j'ai travaillé une demi-heure, les idées s'embrouillent et se troublent en même temps que la vue, et l'action même d'écrire m'est très difficile, les mouvements de la main obéissant mal à la Pensée.

[as soon as I've done half an hour's work, the ideas become muddled and cloudy at the same time as my sight, and even the action of writing is difficult for me, the movements of the hand badly obeying the Mind.] ⁵⁴

So work on his novel went ever more slowly and painfully and, even before he departed Paris for Nice, Maupassant was pushing his spring finishing date for *The Angelus* back to autumn.[55] The more amenable climate in Nice failed to prevent migraines and further eye troubles—Maupassant was incapable of working and wrote to his publisher, Paul Ollendorff, informing him that he could fix no date for completion of *The Angelus*.[56]

In June, Maupassant was in Avignon where, according to the testimony of his valet, François, whilst out sightseeing, he found in the reliquary of a church the inspiration for the physical appearance of *The Angelus*' heroine.[57] For the rest of the summer Maupassant was taking the waters at Divonne-les-Bains in the Jura mountains with occasional stints at a rival hydrotherapy establishment at Champel-les-Bains, not far away in Geneva, Switzerland. It was during one of these sojourns at Champel-les-Bains, in early August, that Maupassant read the manuscript of his work-in-progress to the poet Auguste Dorchain.[58] In September, Maupassant was in Aix-les-Bains where he again recounted *The Angelus*, this time to his mother.[59] In October, writing to an unknown recipient, probably the editor of a literary review, Maupassant confirmed that he had given up writing short stories, wishing only to work on novels from now on:

> j'ai réfléchi et je me suis absolument décidé à ne plus faire de contes ni de nouvelles. C'est usé, fini, ridicule. J'en ai trop fait d'ailleurs. Je ne veux travailler qu'à mes romans, et ne pas distraire mon cerveau par des historiettes de la seule besogne qui me passionne.

> [I have reflected and have absolutely decided not to do any more short stories or novellas. It's over, finished, ridiculous. I've got too much on besides. I only want to work on my novels and not distract my brain with little stories from the only work I'm passionate about.][60]

But by the end of the month, writing to his publisher, Paul Ollendorff, it was not *The Angelus* that he wanted to announce as his next publication, but instead a volume of literary criticism and reminiscences, largely recycled from journalism and essays he had published years earlier.[61] François Tassart tells us that on November 2, now settled in an apartment in Cannes, 'Quant à lui, il a repris son

Angelus, auquel il travaille avec une lenteur obstinée' ['According to him, he has resumed his *Angelus*, on which he works with obstinate slowness'].[62] And it seems that with this stubborn futility, Maupassant would continue to attempt to progress with *The Angelus* right up until his attempted suicide on New Year's Day, 1892.[63] Some newspaper reports of the time even allege that it was frustration at his inability to write and the lack of headway he was making with *The Angelus* that was the immediate trigger for Maupassant's suicide attempt:

De son côté, *le Littoral de Cannes* donne, sur la tentative de suicide de M. de Maupassant, des détails qui confirment ceux que nous avons donnés:

Samedi, à dix heures du soir, M. de Maupassant voulut se remettre à son roman, *l'Angelus*, abandonné depuis quelques jours par suite d'un peu de fatigue cérébrale.

Après un quart d'heure d'efforts surhumains, ne pouvant y parvenir, une nuit profonde se faisant dans son cerveau, il se leva en proie à une surexcitation effrayante, frappa un violent coup de poing sur la table et prononça ces mots à haute voix:

«Puisqu'il en est ainsi, mieux vaut encore mourir. Allons! encore un homme au rancart!»

Et, saisissant un rasoir déposé dans son cabinet de toilette, il se porta un coup à la gorge.

[For its part, *le Littoral de Cannes* gives some details that confirm what we have reported on M. de Maupassant's suicide attempt:

On Saturday, at ten in the evening, M. de Maupassant wanted to resume work on his novel, *The Angelus*, abandoned for a few days as a result of a bit of mental fatigue.

After a quarter of an hour of superhuman efforts without getting anywhere, a dark night descending upon his brain, he stood up, prey to a frightening overexcitement, and, with a violent blow of his fist on the table, loudly pronounced these words:

'If it's going to be like this, better still to die. Go on then! another man for the scrapheap!'

And, seizing a razor from his bathroom, he slashed his throat.][64]

For Maupassant *The Angelus* was meant to be 'the crowning of [his] literary career',[65] the *chef-d'oeuvre* of which he told his mother 'je marche dans mon livre comme dans ma chambre' ['I roam about my book as though in my room'].[66] He seemed to have the story all mapped out in his head and, judging from the accounts of Auguste Dorchain, Hermine Lecomte du Noüy and Madame de Maupassant, he had developed the plot far beyond the opening chapter and few fragments of the surviving manuscript.[67] However he just couldn't seem to get the ideas to flow out from his mind down the hand via the pen and on to the paper. This must have been especially frustrating for a writer as prolific as Maupassant who, so it is said, once wrote a fourteen-thousand word short story in four days, the piece coming out fully formed and direct on to the page, clean as a whistle, no messy deletions, insertions or crossings out at all.[68] The novel remained trapped in his mind, like a piece of phlegm in the throat, particularly hard to dislodge. Maupassant's literary coughs and splutters provided no relief and the final page of the surviving manuscript of *The Angelus*—the last fiction Maupassant wrote—full of scruffy struck through passages, words deleted and reinserted, shows how tortuous the writing process had become for him who had once found it ever so easy, issuing nearly his entire literary corpus in a productive ten-year period.

Nevertheless, in spite of Maupassant's difficulties in composing it, the surviving parts of *The Angelus* are steeped in the clarity and precision of prose that characterized his greatest works. We'll never know if *The Angelus* would have been his crowning masterpiece, but it could have been his *summa*, encapsulating and summarizing the themes, locations and imagery that predominate in his *oeuvre*. Set in Normandy during the Franco-Prussian War, Maupassant's final literary endeavour takes us back to the time and place of 'Boule de suif', the story that signalled his literary breakthrough in 1880, and *The Angelus* thus neatly, sadly and presciently bookends Maupassant's career. Scattered throughout its plans and pages are the seeds of many of Maupassant's overriding thematic concerns and motifs: the horrors and pointlessness of war; brotherly rivalry; the sanctified and wounded mother (both physically and emotionally); the strength of love between mother and son; absent fathers; the shackles of marriage; thwarted ambitions; avarice; cruelty and the malevolence of the universe; muddled religious beliefs; priests with pasts; the impoverishment of our physical senses; doctors and the advances of medical science; tempting female servants; deracination; the Norman countryside; the river Seine; spa towns; snow and winter landscapes.

As such there are plenty of echoes of Maupassant's previous literary successes. The opening passage of *The Angelus* with its lavish description of the château du Bec and its furnishings is reminiscent of *Les Peuples* in *Une Vie* and there are further similarities between that novel's heroine, Jeanne de Lamare, and *The Angelus*'s Countess de Brémontal. [69] Meanwhile the Prussians' invasion of the château and their demands to see its mistress hark back to Maupassant's war stories 'Mademoiselle Fifi' and 'La Folle'. [70] The two brothers in *The Angelus*, Henri and André, of very different temperaments, competing for the affections of the same girl, remind us of Maupassant's fourth novel *Pierre et Jean*. Whilst Maupassant's use of the cold snow-covered Norman countryside as an emblem of the heroine's alienation and vulnerability was a device used adeptly in his earlier stories 'Boule de suif' and 'Première neige'. [71]

For all of its familiar content, *The Angelus* was nevertheless taking Maupassant into new territory. From the outlines of the plot as reported by Dorchain, Lecomte du Noüy and Mme de Maupassant, and from the surviving fragments of text after chapter one, it seems that *The Angelus* was going to be a highly ambitious allegory of Christianity—a skewed, forsaken Christianity imbued with Maupassant's Schopenhauerian pessimism, a Christianity closer to that of Gnosticism than Catholicism, in which the Man-God is betrayed into a world of suffering by a malicious creator god. *The Angelus* would be Maupassant's final howl into the abyss, an ultra-bleak tale in which all the characters suffer, unconsciously tormenting one another, their actions and words, even when originating in love and compassion, ultimately causing further misery. And so even the usually precious bond between mother and son is profaned in *The Angelus* as Maupassant sets about outlining the 'pointlessness and tyranny of devotion'. [72] The Countess de Brémontal's devotion to her crippled son, André, is unable to protect him and, as he suffers, she suffers in turn and her faith, her devotion to God, is undermined. The Abbé Marvaux's devotion in educating André and Dr Paturel's devotion in trying to cure him likewise fail, whilst the doctor's filial

The Foreign Soul and The Angelus

devotion to his mother only sees him frustrated as his career stagnates and stalls in the provinces.

The Angelus is named after the Christan devotion that celebrates the Annunciation of the Incarnation by the angel Gabriel to Mary (Luke 1: 28-38). It is recited three times a day, morning (6.00 a.m.), noon and night (6.00 p.m.), accompanied by the ringing of the Angelus bell, a triple stroke repeated three times, often known in France as the 'peace bell'. After the versicles and responses, the angelus closes with the following prayer:

> Pour forth, we beseech thee, O Lord, thy grace into our hearts; that we, to whom the Incarnation of Christ, thy Son, was made known by the message of an angel, may by his Passion and Cross be brought to the glory of his Resurrection. Through the same Christ, our Lord. Amen. [73]

The angelus of Maupassant's title becomes an ironic reference, a 'peace bell' rung out at a time of war and national misery, its chimes, as Louis Forestier points out, less looking forward to redemption and resurrection than to the pain, crucifixion and death beforehand. [74] It would have been a novel unrelenting and unremitting in its chronicling of human distress, so much so that Auguste Dorchain thought its author, were he to write it as he intended, would be 'powerfully and desperately crushed, like a diver who drowns, by the sinister substance of his thought'. Perhaps the desired depths of pessimism in *The Angelus* would be almost impossible to obtain, mused Dorchain, and Maupassant would ultimately 'come back up again in one movement towards the light and towards hope'? [75] It seems unlikely, but Dorchain's theory may account for the bouts of religious mania Maupassant is said to have experienced after he was interned in Dr Blanche's clinic in Passy in January, 1892. [76]

Ambitious in its form of an allegory of Christianity and an ironic take on the symbolism of the angelus (one wonders if Maupassant would have taken from the thrice-repeated triple peal of the angelus the structure of his novel, three parts of three chapters each?), *The Angelus* was also to take on the classic confrontation between the man of science and man of religion. This clash had been explored by Maupassant's literary masters, Flaubert and Zola; Flaubert, in *Madame Bovary* (1857), putting the pharmacist Homais up against the Abbé Bournisien; Zola, in

Introduction

Pot-Bouille (1882), juxtaposing Dr Juillerat and Abbé Mauduit.[77] It would have been fascinating to see how Maupassant would have developed this contest between science and faith, Dr Paturel and Abbé Marvaux competing over the soul and mind of young André. The small fragment that we have (Fragment III herein) is a tantalizing appetizer, its dialogue reminiscent at times of Dostoevsky.

Maupassant said that *The Angelus* would be a short work,[78] but it was certainly big in scope, perhaps to its own undoing. It's a great shame that Maupassant could not progress with and complete *The Angelus*, but it is also almost fitting and self-fulfilling that a novel with such pessimism and despair at its heart should be left unfinished, its author being carried off by pain and madness into death.

Be it da Vinci's sketches, the fugues of Bach, Coleridge's 'Kubla Khan' or the novels of Kafka, there is something intrinsically melancholy and forlorn about an unfinished work, especially one whose completion was prevented by the author's premature death, the incomplete text mirroring the incomplete life. Posthumously, the fragments passed down to us seem to contain so much potential and leave us sighing unrequited 'What Ifs' and 'If Onlys'; they carry the weight of our unfulfilled hopes and expectations; they are laced with mystery and a baleful quality that leaves us wondering whether they destroyed or hastened the demise of their author. Did the creators burden themselves with tasks too vast to be consigned to canvas, stone or paper, or were their flagons of time emptied just too soon? Either way we are left pondering 'The sadness of the incomplete—the sadness that is often Life, but should never be Art'.[79] Alas that was the fate to befall Maupassant's *The Foreign Soul* and *The Angelus*, but it shouldn't detract from our enjoyment and appreciation of them.

Notes

[1] Guy de Maupassant, letter to Maître Jacob, December 5, 1891, in *Correspondance*, ed. Jacques Suffel, 3 vols. (Geneva: Edito Service, 1973), vol. III, letter no. 741. All translations mine unless stated otherwise.

[2] Francis Steegmuller, *Maupassant* (London: Collins, 1950), p. 251.

³ Maupassant, letter to his mother (Laure de Maupassant), end of September 1887 (*Correspondance*, vol. II, no. 468).
⁴ Maupassant, letter to Ferdinand Brunetière, August 17, 1889 (*Correspondance*, vol. III, no. 566).
⁵ Maupassant, 'Le Roman', p. 714, in *Romans*, ed. Louis Forestier, Bibliothèque de la Pléiade series (Paris: Éditions Gallimard, 1987).
⁶ Paul Ignotus, *The Paradox of Maupassant* (London: University of London Press Ltd, 1966), p. 236.
⁷ The dating of Maupassant's stay in Aix-les-Bains in 1890 is uncertain: Maupassant's valet, François Tassart, places it in July, in his *Souvenirs sur Guy de Maupassant par François son valet de chambre (1883-1893)* (Paris: Plon-Nourrit et Cie, 1911), ch. XV (see also p. 25 herein for an English translation of the relevant passage); however, Maupassant's correspondence seems to suggest that he was in Aix-les-Bains in June and then again, later in the summer, in August-September, having in the interim spent periods in Paris (where he moved apartments), Plombières, Gérardmer and Étretat.
⁸ Queen Victoria, for example, visited Aix-les-Bains, one of her favourite towns, in May, 1890.
⁹ For more on the history and culture of Aix-les-Bains and France's other spa towns in the nineteenth century, see Douglas Peter Mackaman's excellent *Leisure Settings: Bourgeois Culture, Medicine, and the Spa in Modern France* (Chicago and London: The University of Chicago Press, 1998). For more in depth studies of life at spa towns and hydrotherapy establishments by Maupassant, see his novel *Mont-Oriol* (Paris: Victor Havard, 1887), and short story, 'At the Spas', in *To the Sun*, tr. James Wilson (London: Duchy of Lambeth, 2008).
¹⁰ Paul Ignotus, *The Paradox of Maupassant*, p. 155.
¹¹ A new translation of *Notre coeur* by Richard Pevsner, under the title of *Alien Hearts* is due for publication by New York Review of Books in 2009. The best existing translation is probably that of Marjorie Laurie, *Notre Coeur* (London: T Werner Laurie LTD., 1949).
¹² Maupassant, *Notre coeur*, pt. III, ch. III, p. 1179 in *Romans*, ed. Louis Forestier.
¹³ Maupassant, *The Foreign Soul*, p. 22, herein.
¹⁴ Maupassant, *Notre coeur*, pt. II, ch. VII, p. 1136.
¹⁵ Cf. ibid., pt. III, ch. I, pp. 1155-6, 1158-60; and Maupassant, *The Foreign Soul*, pp. 11, 16.

[16] Paul Bourget, 'An Unfinished Novel by Maupassant', p. 37, herein.
[17] Maupassant, *Notre coeur*, pt. III, ch. I, pp. 1150-1.
[18] Maupassant, *The Foreign Soul*, pp. 22-3.
[19] Maupassant, *Notre coeur*, pt. II, ch. I, p. 1078.
[20] Ibid., pt. I, ch. II, p. 1056.
[21] Ibid., pt. II, ch. V, p. 1122.
[22] Maupassant, *The Foreign Soul*, p. 20.
[23] Cf. Maupassant, *Notre coeur*, pt. I, ch. I, pp. 1033-4; and *The Foreign Soul*, p. 7.
[24] Cf. Maupassant, *Notre coeur*, pt. I, ch. I, p. 1046; and *The Foreign Soul*, p. 12.
[25] Maupassant, *Notre coeur*, pt. II, ch. III, p. 1101; and *The Foreign Soul*, p. 11.
[26] A Prince Epilati appears in *Notre coeur*, pt. II, ch. VII, p. 1143; the Marquise Epilati features in *The Foreign Soul*, pp. 11, 14. Another 'petit prince Epilati' appears in *Fort comme la mort*, pt. II, ch. V, p. 991 in *Romans*, ed. Louis Forestier.
[27] In *Notre coeur*, pt. I, ch. I, p. 1046, after making a good first impression in his début conversation with Mme de Burne, André Mariolle is invited to join her in a cup of tea; in *The Foreign Soul*, p. 14, Robert Mariolle receives the same invitation from the Princess de Guerche, after making a similarly good impression in conversation.
[28] *Notre coeur*, pt. III, ch. II, pp. 1166-7; *The Foreign Soul*, p. 9.
[29] Maupassant, letter to his mother, February 22, 1891 (*Correspondance*, vol. III, no. 671). Maupassant began work on *Fort comme la mort* in May 1888.
[30] Steegmuller, *Maupassant*, p. 292.
[31] André's surname in *Notre coeur* seems to have been, at first, Landely, then Maltry, before finally becoming Mariolle. The character of Georges de Maltry originally had the surname of de Millivaudan.
[32] Paul Bourget, 'An Unfinished Novel by Maupassant', p. 36, herein.
[33] p. 79, herein.
[34] *Notre coeur* is widely considered to be a *roman-à-clef*, Michèle de Burne being said to be based variously on Marie Kann, Hermine Lecomte du Noüy, Countess Emmanuela Potocka, Mme Geneviève Straus and Gisèle d'Estoc, or as an amalgamation of several of Maupassant's mistresses. The character of the writer Gaston Lamarthe is said to be based on Paul Bourget and Prédolé the sculptor on Auguste Rodin.
[35] In 1888 Maupassant adapted his story 'Au bord du lit' for the stage as *La paix du ménage*, although it wasn't performed until March 6, 1893, at the Théâtre Français, Paris; Maupassant's play, *Musotte*, written with Jacques Normand, was an adaptation

of his short story 'L'Enfant', and premièred at the Théâtre du Gymnase, Paris, on March 4, 1891; he also started writing a play based on 'Yvette' in 1891. 'Le Horla' was rewritten and published in three different versions: 'Lettre d'un fou', in *Gil Blas*, February 17, 1885; 'Le Horla', in *Gil Blas*, October 26, 1886; and 'Le Horla', in Maupassant's short story collection *Le Horla* (Paris: Ollendorff, 1887). In another example of Maupassant intentionally rewriting and adapting material, we can mention the stories 'Histoire corse' (which first appeared in *Gil Blas*, December 1, 1881); 'Par un soir de printemps' (*Le Gaulois*, May 7, 1881); 'Le Lit' (*Gil Blas*, March 16, 1882, then in *Mademoiselle Fifi*); 'Le Saut du berger' (*Gil Blas*, March 9, 1882); 'Rencontre' (*Le Gaulois*, March 26, 1882); 'Vieux objets' (*Gil Blas*, March 29, 1882); 'la Veillée' (*Gil Blas*, June 7, 1882); and 'Humble drame' (*Gil Blas*, October 2, 1883) which were all extracted from *Une Vie*, the novel Maupassant had started writing in 1877 and that was serialized in *Gil Blas* from February 27 to April 6, 1883 before then being published in book form by Victor Havard.

[36] *Notre coeur* was first published in the *Revue des Deux Mondes*, May 15, June 1 and June 15, 1890, before being published in book form later in June by Ollendorff.

[37] Charles Lapierre, 'Souvenirs Intimes', in *Journal des Débats*, August 10, 1893, quoted in Steegmuller, *Maupassant*, p. 286; Louis Forestier, 'Notice' to *Notre coeur*, in *Romans*, p. 1624.

[38] Maupassant, letter to Ferdinand Brunetière, March, 1887 (*Correspondance*, vol. II, no. 451).

[39] Maupassant, letter to Ferdinand Brunetière, December, 1887 (*Correspondance*, vol. II, no. 474). The novel Maupassant speaks of is *Pierre et Jean*.

[40] Maupassant, letter to Victor Havard, received January 2, 1889 (*Correspondance*, vol. III, no. 538).

[41] Maupassant, letter to Ferdinand Brunetière, August, 1889 (*Correspondance*, vol. III, no. 565).

[42] Maupassant, letter to Ferdinand Brunetière, August 17, 1889 (*Correspondance*, vol. III, no. 566). The piece intended for *Le Figaro* was probably 'Le Champ d'oliviers', the only short story Maupassant published in *Le Figaro* after this letter was written, appearing in the issues of February 14 and 23, 1890, later being included in the collection *L'Inutile Beauté* (Paris: Victor Havard, 1890). I presume that the manuscript Maupassant mentions he will give to Brunetière is that of the work he has titled *The Foreign Soul*, rather than the piece for *Le Figaro*.

⁴³ Maupassant, letter to Ferdinand Brunetière, November 18, 1889 (*Correspondance*, vol. III, no. 576). Guy was tasked with the unenviable duty of delivering his insane brother, Hervé, into the care an asylum in Bron, near Lyons, in August, 1889. Hervé died there not long after on November 13.

⁴⁴ See the accounts of Tassart and Mme de Maupassant herein, pp. 25-8 and 79. In addition, Tassart writes in his *Souvenirs*, ch. XVI, p. 248, in an entry dated August 6, 1890: 'Dans la voiture, en cours de route, il m'annonça sans préambule qu'il avait commencé l'*Ame étrangère* et qu'il croyait que ce serait un bon roman, un peu sensationnel peut-être.' ['In the carriage, during the journey, he informed me without preamble that he had begun *The Foreign Soul* and that he believed it would be a good novel, perhaps even a little sensational.']

⁴⁵ One of which might have been Maupassant's relationship with Marie Kann, one of his mistresses, whom Maupassant is said to have shared with his friend, the writer and critic Paul Bourget. Perhaps this explains why André Mariolle in *Notre coeur* is never entirely sure how deep Michèle de Burne's relationships with the other male members of her salon run, and also the beginning of Robert Mariolle's relationship with Henriette Lambel, when he is seeing her at the same time as one of his friends.

⁴⁶ See herein, pp. 25-6.

⁴⁷ Ibid., pp. 19-23.

⁴⁸ See p. 79, herein. Carmen Sylva was the literary alias of Pauline Elisabeth Ottilie Luise zu Wied (1843-1916), the German-born Queen Elisabeth of Romania, the wife of King Carol I (1839-1914, r. 1881-1914). She was the author of poems, plays, novels and short stories as well as translations into German.

⁴⁹ These sources—François Tassart's accounts of research in Aix-les-Bains and of Alexandre Dumas fils' involvement in plot development, and Mme de Maupassant's account—are translated herein, pp. 25-8, 29-32, and 79.

⁵⁰ See herein, p. 37.

⁵¹ See n. 44 above.

⁵² Cf. Tassart, *Souvenirs*, ch. XVII, p. 265: 'A partir de ce moment il laisse de côté l'*Ame étrangère* et ne travaille plus qu'à un ouvrage unique, son *Angelus*.' ['From this time [the end of February, 1891] he pushed *The Foreign Soul* to one side and worked only on one sole work, his *Angelus*.'] Maupassant was also, at this time, wrapping up his involvement on the play he had written with Jacques Normand, *Musotte*, an adaptation of Maupassant's short story 'L'Enfant', which would premier at the Théâtre

du Gymnase, Paris, on March 4, 1891. Maupassant first mentions *The Angelus* in his correspondence in a letter to his mother, February 22, 1891, where he says that it isn't progressing, but that he will try and finish it in April, when he will be staying in Nice (*Correspondance*, vol. III, no. 671). In a letter to an unknown addressee of October 1891 (*Correspondance*, vol. III, no. 728), Maupassant mentions a work 'à laquelle je travaille depuis deux ans' ['on which I've been working for two years']. This is, undoubtedly, *The Angelus*, and although Maupassant may be exaggerating the timescale, it supports the notion that Maupassant had begun *The Angelus* before 1891.

[53] See Maupassant's letters to his mother for February 22 and March, 1891 (*Correspondance*, vol. III, nos. 671 and 675).

[54] Maupassant, letter to his mother, February 22, 1891 (*Correspondance*, vol. III, no. 671).

[55] Maupassant, letter to his mother, March 26, 1891 (*Correspondance*, vol. III, no. 684).

[56] Maupassant, letter to Paul Ollendorff, April, 1891 (*Correspondance*, vol. III, no. 692).

[57] See herein, pp. 81-2. The woman is, presumably, Mme de Brémontal.

[58] See herein, pp. 69-71.

[59] See herein, p. 79.

[60] Maupassant, letter to unknown recipient, October, 1891 (*Correspondance*, vol. III, no. 728).

[61] Maupassant, letter to Paul Ollendorff, October 28, 1891 (*Correspondance*, vol. III, no. 730):

> ...Il faut que je vous voie demain. Je vais avoir un volume presque tout de suite, qui est, non pas mon roman, mais un livre de critique et portraits en quatre parties:
>
> *Études sur Flaubert*, parue 2 fois (Préface des *Lettres à Madame Sand* et *Bouvard et Pécuchet* - Œuvres complètes). J'y ajouterai l'article de documents intimes publié à l'inauguration de son monument je ne sais plus où, *Gaulois*, *Gil Blas* ou *Écho de Paris*, l'année dernière le 23 novembre.
>
> BOUILHET. - Je vais donner dans quelques jours au Figaro un grand article sur ce poète méconnu, avec citations superbes.
>
> TOURGUENEFF. - Choses intimes.
>
> ZOLA. - Paru *Galerie des Hommes célèbres*. Cela à retoucher...

[...I must see you tomorrow. I am going to have a volume ready almost immediately which is, not my novel, but a book of criticism and portraits in four parts.

Études sur Flaubert, published 2 times before (Preface to Lettres à Madame Sand and Bouvard et Pécuchet – Complete works). To which I'll add the article of intimate documents published at the inauguration of his monument, I don't know where, Gaulois, Gil Blas or the Écho de Paris, last year on November 23.

BOUILHET. – In a few days I'm going to give to the Figaro a big article with brilliant citations on this unrecognized poet.

TURGENEV. – Intimate things.

ZOLA. – Published in Galerie des Hommes célèbres. To be amended...]

This volume never appeared and, it seems, Maupassant's new article on Bouilhet was never written, although earlier in his career he did write an article 'Louis Bouilhet', in Le Gaulois, August 21, 1882. The study on Flaubert was 'Gustave Flaubert', in Revue Bleue, January 19 and 25, 1884, also appearing as a preface to Lettres de Gustave Flaubert à George Sand (Paris: Charpentier, 1884) and Gustave Flaubert, Œuvres complètes, vol. VII (Paris: A Quantin, 1885). The additional article on Flaubert was in fact two articles: 'Gustave Flaubert', in L'Écho de Paris, November 24, 1890; and 'Flaubert et sa maison', in the supplement of Gil Blas, November 24, 1890. The piece on Turgenev was probably to be based on his obituaries both entitled 'Ivan Tourgueneff' that were printed in Le Gaulois, September 5, 1883, and Gil Blas, September 6, 1883. The Zola essay, 'Émile Zola' appeared in Revue Bleue, March 10, 1883, whilst also being printed separately as a booklet, Émile Zola, in the 'Célébrités contemporaines' collection (Paris: A Quantin, 1883).

[62] Tassart, Souvenirs, ch. XVIII, p. 288.

[63] Ibid., p. 297: 'Je me représentai qu'il était impossible qu'il nous quittât ainsi, quand, la veille encore, il nous parlait en termes si lucides de ses travaux, de son Moine de Fécamp et de son Angelus.' ['I told myself that it was impossible that he'd leave us like that when, only the evening before, he was speaking to us in such lucid terms about his works, his Moine de Fécamp and his Angelus.'] Maupassant never wrote the intended nouvelle 'Le Moine de Fécamp'.

[64] Ch. Demailly, 'M. Ollendorff et M. de Maupassant', in Le Gaulois, Wednesday, January 6, 1892. The same report from the Littoral de Cannes, edited by M. Gautier,

the owner of the villa in which Maupassant was staying, appeared in 'La Maladie de Guy de Maupassant', in *L'Intransigeant*, Friday, January 8, 1892.

[65] Tassart, *Souvenirs*, ch. XVII, p. 271; see also p. 82 herein.

[66] Maupassant, letter to his mother, quoted in Albert Lumbroso, *Souvenirs sur Maupassant: sa dernière maladie, sa mort* (Rome: Bocca Frères, 1905), vol. I, p. 118. A variation of this quotation is given in Edmond de Goncourt's *Edmond et Jules de Goncourt. Journal, mémoires de la vie littéraire, 1851-1896*, ed. Robert Ricatte (Paris: Flammarion, 1959), in an entry for Sunday, October 1, 1893: 'je viens de commencer *L'Angélus*, et jamais je n'ai travaillé avec une facilité pareille, et je marche de plain-pied dans mon livre comme dans mon jardin... Je ne sais pas si mon livre sera un chef-d'œuvre, mais ce sera mon chef-d'œuvre.' ['I have just begun *The Angelus* and I have never before worked with such ease, I roam about my book at ground level as though in my garden... I don't know if my book will be a masterpiece, but it will be my masterpiece.'] Goncourt is quoting a letter Maupassant wrote to his mother, read by her to Paul Alexis and in turn reported by him to Goncourt.

[67] These accounts are contained herein, pp. 69-79. Louis Ganderax, editor of the *Revue de Paris* who first published *The Angelus*, mentions in his article 'Pour Maupassant', in *Le Gaulois*, Monday, January 11, 1892, another person to whom Maupassant recounted *The Angelus*, the French playwright, Georges de Porto-Riches (1849-1930): '*l'Angelus*,—un de ses plus beaux récits, m'a dit Georges de Porto-Riche, à qui, d'un bout à l'autre, il l'avait raconté.' ['*The Angelus*,—one of his most beautiful pieces, Georges de Porto-Riches told me, to whom he had recounted it from start to finish.'] Dorchain and Lecomte du Noüy's testimonies also suggest that not only had Maupassant conceived the plot of *The Angelus* as a whole, but that he had also written down more portions than the 41 pages of manuscript that have passed down to us.

[68] Robert Harborough Sherard, *The Life, Work and Evil Fate of Guy de Maupassant* (New York: Brentanos, n.d.), p. 360, quoted in Deborah Hayden, 'Guy de Maupassant and Friedrich Nietzsche. A Comparison of Two Cases of 19th-Century General Paresis', in J Bogousslavsky and F Boller (eds.), *Neurological Disorders in Famous Artists* (Basel: Karger Publishers, 2005), p. 13.

[69] Their youths and upbringings in particular share common ground: Both their mothers were brought up in atheistic surroundings, but nevertheless had a respect for the Church. Both girls, Jeanne de Lamare and Germaine Boutemart were sent away to be educated by ecclesiastical figures until ready to return to Normandy and plans for marriage.

Both girls are romantic dreamers with a fondness for reading and roaming the countryside. And both desire to have daughters, turning to religion when their longings for a second child appear to be frustrated.

70 'Mademoiselle Fifi' first appeared in *Gil Blas*, March 23, 1882, before being included in the collection of the same name; 'La Folle' was first published in *Le Gaulois*, December 5, 1882, before being included in the collection *Contes de la bécasse* (Paris: Rouveyre et Blond, 1883).

71 'Première neige' was first published in *Le Gaulois*, December 11, 1883.

72 Paul Ignotus, *The Paradox of Maupassant*, p. 238.

73 *Compendium of the Catechism of the Catholic Church* (London: Catholic Truth Society, 2006), p. 180.

74 Louis Forestier, 'Notice' to *L'Angélus*, in *Romans*, p. 1683.

75 See herein, pp. 70-1.

76 For example, Maupassant wanted to have his confession heard: see Georges Normandy, *La Fin de Maupassant* (Paris: Albin Michel, 1927), p. 194; and François Tassart, *Nouveaux souvenirs intimes sur Guy de Maupassant (inédits)*, ed. Pierre Cogny (Paris: A G Nizet, 1962), ch. XVI. It should be noted that Maupassant also frequently railed against and quarrelled with God during his internment in Passy: see Normandy, *La Fin de Maupassant*, pp. 214, 215, 218, 220, 225, 228, 230, 233.

77 It is worth noting that there is a character named Abbé Mauduit in Maupassant's story 'Après', first published posthumously in the collection *Le Colporteur* (Paris: Ollendorff, 1900). 'Après' was probably written in 1891 and shares several features in common with *The Angelus*, the abbé's gloomy sensitivity and foreboding finding a counterpart in the Countess de Brémontal, and his view of life as a sequence of unbearable pains and struggles being a sentiment paralleled in the pages of Maupassant's unfinished novel.

78 Maupassant, letter to his mother, March, 1891 (*Correspondance*, vol. III, no. 675): 'J'en ai fait très peu, mais il sera court' ['I have done very little, but it will be short'].

79 E M Forster, *A Room with a View* (London: Penguin, 2000), pt. II, ch. 11, p. 113.

Select Bibliography

Editions of *The Foreign Soul* and *The Angelus*

French

L'Angélus, manuscript, box 13, folder 4 of 'Series II: French Literary Manuscripts Collected by Artine Arinian, 1785-1958', in Artine Artinian Collection, at the Harry Ransom Humanities Research Center, the University of Texas at Austin.

L'Ame étrangère, in *La Revue de Paris*, November 15, 1894, pp. 225-45.

L'Angélus, in *La Revue de Paris*, April 1, 1895, pp. 449-72.

L'Ame étrangère and *L'Angélus*, in *Oeuvres posthumes*, vol. II (1910), = vol. XXIX of *Oeuvres complètes de Guy de Maupassant*, ed. Pol Neveux, 29 vols. (Paris: Louis Conard, 1908-10), 233 pp. AE and AN with the short story 'Les Dimanches d'un bourgeois de Paris', the *chronique* 'La Vie d'un paysagiste', and the essay 'Étude sur Gustave Flaubert'.

L'Ame étrangère and *L'Angélus*, vol. XIII (1935), ill. Gérard Cochet, w. 'Notice' by René Dumesnil, of *Oeuvres complètes illustrées de Guy de Maupassant*, ed. René Dumesnil and Jean Loize, 15 vols. (Paris: Librairie de France, 1934-8), 331 pp. AE and AN with *Fort comme la mort*.

L'Angélus, in *Romans*, ed. Albert-Marie Schmidt (Paris: A Michel, 1959), 1415 pp. AN with Maupassant's six completed novels.

L'Ame étrangère and *L'Angélus*, vol. XII (1962), ill. Ferdinand Bac / engraved by G Lemoine, of *Oeuvres complètes*, ed. Gilbert Sigaux, 16 vols. (Lausanne: Editions Rencontre, 1961-2), 511 pp. AE and AN with *Notre coeur* and 'L'inutile beauté'.

L'Ame étrangère and *L'Angélus*, in *La Main gauche; L'Inutile beauté; Contes divers; Fragments*, vol. XI (1971), ill. Lise Luce Baudin, of *Oeuvres complètes de Maupassant*, ed. Pascal Pia, 17 vols. (Evreux: Le Cercle du Bibliophile, 1969-73), 433 pp.

L'Ame étrangère and *L'Angélus*, in *Romans*, ed. Louis Forestier (Paris: Gallimard 'Bibliothèque de la Pléiade', 1987), 1705 pp. AE and AN together with Maupassant's six completed novels. Forestier presents each novel with an introduction, note to the text, bibliography and endnotes, also recording manuscript variants.

L'Angélus in *Boule de suif et autres histoires de guerre*, ed. Antonia Fonyi (Paris: Flammarion, 1991), 315 pp. AN with the short stories 'Boule de suif', 'Mademoiselle Fifi', 'Deux amis', 'Le Père Milon', 'La Moustache', 'Un duel', 'Un coup d'État', 'La Mère sauvage', 'L'Horrible', 'Les Idées du colonel', 'Le Lit 29', 'Les Prisonniers', 'Les Rois', 'Le Mariage du lieutenant Laré', 'Souvenir', and the *chroniques* 'Les Soirées de Médan', and 'La Guerre' and full critical apparatus.

L'Angélus in *Récits de guerre et de défaite, suivis de L'Angélus*, vol. 14 (1993), of *Contes et romans*, ed. Georges Belle, 14 vols. (Paris: France Loisirs, 1992-4), 283 pp.

L'Ame étrangère in *Notre cœur, suivi de L'Ame étrangère*, vol. 13 (1994), of *Contes et romans*, ed. Georges Belle, 14 vols. (Paris: France Loisirs, 1992-4), 268 pp.

L'Ame étrangère and *L'Angélus*, in *Les romans*, ed. Claude Aziza (Paris: Omnibus, 1999), 1353 pp. AE and AN together with Maupassant's six completed novels; various short stories and articles by Maupassant related to the themes of his novels; articles by Maupassant on writing and literature; articles by Maupassant about the society of his time; reviews and articles on Maupassant's novels by other writers; a chronology of Maupassant's life and times; and a select filmography of cinematic adaptations of Maupassant's work.

Biographies and Studies of Maupassant in English

Artinian, Artine, *Maupassant Criticism in France (1880-1940)* (New York: King's Crown Press, 1941), 228 pp.

Select Bibliography

Artinian, Artine, and Artinian, Robert Willard, *Maupassant Criticism: A Centennial Bibliography, 1880-1979* (Jefferson, NC: McFarland, 1982), 178 pp.

Ball, Bertrand Logan, *Love and Nature, Unity and Doubling in the Novels of Maupassant*, ed. Helen Roulston, American University Studies, Series II: Romance Languages and Literature, vol. 79 (New York: Peter Lang, 1988), 152 pp.

Boyd, Ernest, *Guy de Maupassant: A Biographical Study* (London and New York: Alfred A Knopf, 1926), 258 pp.

Bryant, David, *The Rhetoric of Pessimism and Strategies of Containment in the Short Stories of Guy de Maupassant*, vol. 7 of Studies in French Literature (Lewinston, NY, Lampeter, Wales, and Queenston, Canada: The Edwin Mellen Press, 1993), 190 pp.

Coulter, Stephen, *Damned shall be Desire: The Passionate Life of Guy de Maupassant* (London: Jonathan Cape, 1958), 350 pp. A novelization of Maupassant's life.

Donaldson-Evans, Mary, *A Woman's Revenge: The Chronology of Dispossession in Maupassant's fiction* (Lexington, KY: French Forum, Publishers, 1986), 159 pp.

Dugan, John Raymond, *Illusion and Reality: A Study of Descriptive Techniques in the Works of Guy de Maupassant* (The Hague and Paris: Mouton, 1973), 209 pp.

Fusco, Richard, *Maupassant and the American Short Story: The Influence of Form at the Turn of the Century* (University Park, PA: Pennsylvania State University Press, 1994), 230 pp.

Gregorio, Laurence A, *Maupassant's Fiction and the Darwinian View of Life* (New York and Oxford: Peter Lang, 2005), 200 pp.

Harris, Trevor A Le V, *Maupassant in the Hall of Mirrors: Ironies of Repetition in the Work of Guy de Maupassant* (Basingstoke: Macmillan, 1990), 230 pp.

Hartig, Rachel Mildred, *Struggling under the Destructive Glance: Androgyny in the Novels of Guy de Maupassant* (New York: P Lang, 1991), 134 pp.

Ignotus, Paul, *The Paradox of Maupassant* (London: University of London Press Ltd, 1966), 288 pp.

Jackson, Stanley, *Guy de Maupassant* (London: Duckworth, 1938), 310 pp.

Kirkbride, Ronald de Levington, *The Private Life of Guy de Maupassant* (New York: Sears Publishing Co., 1932), 252 pp.

Lerner, Michael G, *Maupassant* (London: George Allen & Unwin Ltd, 1975), 301 pp.

Macnamara, Matthew, *Style and vision in Maupassant's Nouvelles* (Berne and New York: P Lang, 1986), 247 pp.

Niess, Robert J, 'Autobiographical Symbolism in Maupassant's Last works', in *Symposium*, no. 14, Autumn 1960.

Poteau-Tralie, Mary L, *Voices of Authority. Criminal Obsession in Guy de Maupassant's Short Works* (New York: Peter Lang, 1994), 146 pp.

Ramsey, John Anglin, *The Literary Doctrines of Flaubert, Maupassant, and Zola: A Comparative Study* (University of Illinois thesis, 1957), 283 pp.

Sherard, Robert Harborough, *The Life, Work and Evil Fate of Guy de Maupassant (Gentilhomme de lettres)* (London: T Werner Laurie LTD., 1926), 399 pp.

Steegmuller, Francis, *Maupassant* (London: Collins, 1950), 384 pp.; repr. as *Maupassant: A Lion in the Path* (London: Macmillan, 1972), 430 pp.

Stivale, Charles J, *The Art of Rupture: Narrative Desire and Duplicity in the Tales of Guy de Maupassant* (Ann Arbor, MI: The University of Michigan Press, 1994, repr. 1997), 264 pp.

Sullivan, Edward D, *Maupassant: The Novelist* (Princeton, NJ: Princeton University Press, 1954), 199 pp.

Sullivan, Edward D, *Maupassant: The Short Stories* (London: Edward Arnold (Publishers) LTD., 1962), 64 pp.

Wallace, A H, *Guy de Maupassant*, Twayne's World Authors Series, no. 265 (New York: Twayne Publishers, Inc., 1973), 156 pp.

Walls, Alison M K, *The Sentiment of Spending: Intimate Relationships and the Consumerist Environment in the Works of Zola, Rachilde, Maupassant, and Huysmans* (New York and Oxford: Peter Lang, 2008), 164 pp.

Studies and Articles with relevance to *The Foreign Soul* and *The Angelus*

(See also the introductions and notes to the editions published by Conard (1910), Librairie de France (1935), and Bibliothèque de la Pléiade (1987), listed above.)

Aius Locutius (pseud. Domenico Lanza), 'L'Angelus di Guy de Maupassant', in *La Gazzetta letteraria*, vol. XVIII, no. 34, August 25, 1894.

Select Bibliography

Aius Locutius (pseud. Domenico Lanza), 'Le opere postume di Guy de Maupassant', in *La Gazzetta letteraria*, vol. XVIII, no. 45, November 10, 1894.

Aius Locutius (pseud. Domenico Lanza), '*L'Ame étrangère*', in *La Gazzetta letteraria*, vol. XVIII, no. 34, December 1, 1894.

Colleville, vicomte de, 'L'oeuvre posthume de Guy de Maupassant', in *Le Figaro*, August 14, 1894.

Donaldson-Evans, Mary, *A Woman's Revenge: The Chronology of Dispossession in Maupassant's fiction* (Lexington, KY: French Forum, Publishers, 1986), pp. 101-3.

Drovetti, G, 'Maupassant e *l'Angelus*', in *Stampa Sera*, August 18-19, 1950.

Gregh, Fernand, 'Les œuvres posthumes de Guy de Maupassant', in *Revue bleue*, vol. XV, April 13, 1901, pp.465-7.

'Les trois versions de *L'Angélus*', in *L'Angélus*, journal de l'association des amis de Maupassant, no. 15, December 2004-January 2005.

Sabelli, Franco, *L'anima estranea e l'Angelus: romanzi frammentari* (Rome: Lux, 1908), 106 pp.

Chronology of Maupassant's Life and Works

1850—August 5, Henry René Albert Guy de Maupassant born at the Château de Miromesnil in Tourville-sur-Arques, near Dieppe, the son of Gustave (1821-99), a notary, and Laure de Maupassant (née Le Poittevin, 1821-1904), a childhood friend of Flaubert (1821-80) and Louis Bouilhet (1822-69).

1854—The Maupassants move to the Château d'Ymauville, in Grainville-Ymauville, near Le Havre.

1856—Birth of Guy's younger brother, Hervé de Maupassant.

1858—The Maupassants spend the summer at the coastal fishing village and resort of Étretat where they buy a house, *Les Verguies*, Laure and Hervé moving there the following year.

1859—Gustave employed at a Paris bank, the family move to Passy.

1859-60—Guy at school at the Lycée Napoléon, Paris.

1860-2—Marriage between Gustave and Laure breaks up, Gustave remains in Paris, Laure moves with the two boys to Étretat.

1863—Guy enrolled at a Catholic boarding school, the Institution Ecclésiastique in Yvetot. Legal separation of Gustave and Laure.

1867—Guy expelled for writing 'obscene' verses. He becomes a boarder at the Lycée Corneille in Rouen, where Bouilhet, a poet and the city librarian, acts as his guardian and encourages his writing.

1868—At Étretat Guy meets Algernon Charles Swinburne (1837-1909), having been in one of the fishing boats that went to the poet's rescue as he was drowning.

1869—Guy receives his *baccalauréat*. Bouilhet introduces Guy to Flaubert. Death of Bouilhet. Guy enrols at law school in Paris.

1870—July 15, France declares war on Prussia, Guy enlists voluntarily. September 1, French defeated at Sedan.

1871—January 28, French surrender, end of Siege of Paris (from September 19, 1870). Paris Commune until May 28. Maupassant discharged from the army in November.

1872—Guy becomes an unsalaried civil servant at the Ministry of the Marine and Colonies, in Paris; he is living in a ground floor flat at 2 rue Moncey, Montmartre. Spends his free time boating along the Seine at Argenteuil, Chatou, Bougival and Sartrouville, a passion that had been engendered in his childhood and would last all his life.

1873—Guy graduates to a paid position at the Ministry. He begins to see more and more of Flaubert, who oversees his literary pursuits.

1875—Publication, under the pseudonym of Joseph Prunier, of his story 'La Main d'écorché' in the provincial paper *Almanach lorrain de Pont-à-Mousson*—Maupassant's first published work. First private performance of his play *À la feuille de rose, maison turque*. Maupassant writes his one-act comedy *Une Répétition* (publ. Paris: Tresse, 1879, in *Saynètes et monologues*, 6th series).

1876—Increasingly a part of the Parisian literary scene, having published some poems, articles and stories under various pseudonyms. Through Flaubert he began to mix in literary circles, including such figures as Émile Zola (1840-1902), Edmond de Goncourt (1822-96), Alphonse Daudet (1840-97), Henry James, jr. (1843-1916), Catulle Mendès (1841-1909), Stéphane Mallarmé (1842-98), Auguste compte de Villiers de L'Isle-Adam (1838-89), and Ivan Turgenev (1818-83). Maupassant becomes a part of the Médan group of writers gathered around Zola, also consisting of Paul Alexis (1847-1901), Joris-Karl Huysmans (1848-1907), Léon Hennique (1851-1935), and Henry Céard (1851-1924). Maupassant starts to write his drama in verse, *La Trahison de la Comtesse de Rhune*. Moves to 17 rue Clauzel, Montmartre.

1877—Second performance of *À la feuille de rose, maison turque*. In August receives leave to visit Switzerland on health grounds, Maupassant aware of his having contracted syphilis. In December begins to plan a novel *Une Vie*.

Chronology

1878—Maupassant transfers to the Ministry of Education.
1879—February 19, Maupassant's play *Histoire du vieux temps* performed in Paris (publ. Paris: Tresse, 1879). September, travels in Brittany.
1880—January, Maupassant ordered to appear before a magistrate for an 'outrage against decency and public morality' regarding the publication of his poem 'Une Fille', in the *Revue moderne et naturaliste*, November 1, 1879. A letter of defence from Flaubert, printed in *Le Gaulois*, February 21, combined with the fact that the poem, with the different title of 'Au bord de l'eau', had already appeared three years earlier without stir in Catulle Mendès' magazine *République des Lettres*, March 20, 1876, meant that the prosecution was dropped by February 27. April, 'Boule de suif' published in *Les Soirées de Médan* (Paris: Charpentier). Also publishes a volume of poetry, *Des Vers* (Paris: Charpentier), and begins to write for *Le Gaulois*. May 8, Death of Flaubert. September-October travels to Corsica. In Paris moves to larger apartment at 83 rue Dulong. Probably around this time that he begins his relationship with Gisèle d'Estoc (pseud. Marie-Paul Desbarres, 1863-1907).
1881—May, publication of *La Maison Tellier* (Paris: Victor Havard), a collection of short stories. July-September, travels in Algeria as correspondent for *Le Gaulois*.
1882—Short story collection *Mademoiselle Fifi* (Bruxelles: Kistemaekers). After a series of periods of extended leave, officially leaves his post at the Ministry of Education to make his living from his writing. Travels in Brittany in the summer.
1883—First novel *Une Vie* published (Paris: Victor Havard). Short story collections *Contes de la bécasse* (Paris: Rouveyre et Blond), *Mademoiselle Fifi, nouveaux contes* (enlarged edition, Paris: Victor Havard). Buys a house which he names *La Guillette* in Étretat. Employs his valet, François Tassart, who stays in his service for the rest of Maupassant's life. July at the watering place of Châtel-Guyon in the Auvergne.
1884—January, *Au soleil* [*To the Sun*] published (Paris: Victor Havard); rents an apartment in Cannes and will henceforth largely divide his time between there, le cap d'Antibes, Étretat and Paris. In Paris moves to 10 rue Montchanin, taking the ground floor of his cousin Louis Le Poittevin's

(1847-1909) house. Short story collections *Clair de Lune* (Paris: E Monnier), *Miss Harriet* (Paris: Victor Havard), *Les Soeurs Rondoli* (Paris: Ollendorff). In this year Maupassant forges many of his more intimate and long-lasting relationships with women: In the spring he spends time in Étretat with Clémence Brun-Chabas, Hermine Lecomte du Noüy (1855-1915), and Blanche Roosevelt Macchetta Tucker (1853-98). Maupassant is a regular at many society salons, being one of the male 'Macchabées' (so-called because they were apparently willing to die for their hostess) gathered around Countess Emmanuela Potocka (née Pignatelli, 1852-1943); he also visits the houses of the Warshawski (*or* Warchawsky) sisters, Loulia Cahen d'Anvers (1854-1918) and Marie Kann (1861-1928)—both of whom may have been his lovers. Maupassant is also introduced to the future Mme Straus (née Geneviève Halévy, 1849-1926).

1885—Second novel *Bel-Ami* (Paris: Victor Havard). Short story collections *Yvette* (Paris: Victor Havard), *Contes du Jour et de la Nuit* (Paris: Marpon et Flammarion), *Contes et nouvelles* (Paris: Charpentier). Travels in Italy (April-May). August takes waters at Châtel-Guyon.

1886—Short story collections *Toine* (Paris: Marpon et Flammarion), *Monsieur Parent* (Paris: Ollendorff), *La Petite Roque* (Paris: Victor Havard), *Contes choisis* (Paris: Librairie illustrée). Travels to England in the spring. January, rents villa in Antibes, from where he goes sailing on his newly purchased yacht the *Bel-Ami* later in the year with his faithful crew of valet François, skipper Bernard and mate Raymond. July at Châtel-Guyon. In summer rents *Maison Fournais* in Chatou.

1887—Third novel *Mont-Oriol* (Paris: Victor Havard). Short story collection *Le Horla* (Paris: Ollendorff). March-April yachting off Antibes in *Bel-Ami*. July 8, hot-air balloon voyage from La Villette to Heyst-sur-Mer in balloon named *Le Horla*. October, travels in Algeria and Tunisia (until January 1888).

1888—Fourth novel *Pierre et Jean* (Paris: Ollendorff). Second travel book *Sur l'eau* (Paris: Marpon et Flammarion). Short story collections *Le Rosier de Madame Husson* (Paris: Quantin), *L'Héritage* (Paris: Marpon et Flammarion). March-April yachting off Cannes in *Bel-Ami*. Worsening health leads to stays at Aix-les-Bains in April and October. June, second balloon voyage in *Le Horla*. October, further travels to North Africa (until January 1889).

1889—Fifth novel *Fort comme la mort* (Paris: Ollendorff). Short story collection *La Main gauche* (Paris: Ollendorff). January, buys new yacht (again renamed *Bel-Ami*) and goes sailing off Italian coast in October. In summer rents villa in Triel-sur-Seine. November 3, death of Hervé de Maupassant, insane, in an asylum. In Paris moves to 14 avenue Victor Hugo.

1890—Third travel book *La Vie errante* (Paris: Ollendorff). Sixth novel *Notre coeur* (Paris: Ollendorff). Short story collections *L'Inutile Beauté* (Paris: Victor Havard), *Histoire d'une fille de ferme* (Paris: Marpon et Flammarion). In Paris moves to 24 rue Boccador. Begins *L'Angélus* [*The Angelus*], a novel that will remain unfinished at Maupassant's death. June-September, staying in Aix-les-Bains, and in Plombières-les-Bains and Gérardmer in the Vosges département. September-November, travels once more to Algeria.

1891—Play *Musotte*, written with Jacques Normand (1848-1931), performed successfully at Théâtre du Gymnase (publ. Paris: Ollendorff, 1891). June-August, staying in Divonne-les-Bains in the Jura mountains. September, at Aix-les-Bains. From November at the Chalet de l'Isère, in Cannes.

1892—Night of January 1/2, attempted suicide in Cannes. January 7 admitted, insane, into Dr Blanche's clinic, in Passy.

1893—March, comedy *La paix de ménage* staged at Théâtre Français (publ. Paris: Ollendorff, 1893). July 6, death of Maupassant. July 8, buried in Montparnasse.

1894—*L'Ame étrangère* [*The Foreign Soul*] first published in the *Revue de Paris*, November 15.

1895—*L'Angélus* first published in the *Revue de Paris*, April 1.

1897—Posthumous collection of stories *Trois contes* (Paris: Gautier).

1899—Posthumous collection of stories *Le Père Milon* (Paris: Ollendorff).

1900—Posthumous collection of stories *Le Colporteur* (Paris: Ollendorff).

Note to the Text

The translations of Maupassant's *L'Ame étrangère* and *L'Angélus* are based on the texts in the Conard edition, that is, *Oeuvres posthumes*, vol. II, ed. Pol Neveux (Paris: Louis Conard, 1910), in consultation with *Oeuvres complètes illustrées de Guy de Maupassant*, vol. XIII, ed. René Dumesnil and Jean Loize (Paris: Librairie de France, 1935) and *Romans*, ed. Louis Forestier (Paris: Gallimard 'Bibliothèque de la Pléiade', 1987). The sources of the texts used for the supplementary material are given in the endnotes.

I have followed the Conard edition in paragraph structure and emphasis (italics, capitals etc.) with some minor deviations in the treatment of titles such as *comtesse*, *marquise*, *princesse*, and *abbé* which have been rendered, where full titles are given, with initial capital letters in their English translations. I have left the ecclesiastical titles of *abbé* and *curé*—both of which roughly equate to the English 'priest' and *abbé* also to 'Father'—in the original French, to reflect the different ways in which Abbé Marvaux is addressed (Maupassant also uses *prêtre* which I have translated as 'priest'). I think on only one occasion have I carried a French word over into the translation and placed it in italics, that being the word *génératrices* in Paul Bourget's essay. Editorial insertions and clarifications appear in square brackets. Some minor manuscript variations of *The Angelus* are included in the Appendix.

I have translated both titles rather literally and my rendering of *L'Ame étrangère* as *The Foreign Soul* perhaps bears some explanation. Paul Ignotus gives a few good possible translations in his *The Paradox of Maupassant* (London: University of London Press Ltd, 1966), p. 237: 'Strange Soul', 'Estranged', 'Alien' or 'Alienated'.

The Foreign Soul and The Angelus

My choice of *The Foreign Soul*, influenced by Paul Bourget's reading, whilst hopefully implying a general 'strangeness' or 'difference' (of man to woman, woman to man, and also of the bourgeois to the aristocratic), also suggests a specific difference of nationality (French to Romanian, say, hinting at Maupassant's future plot direction of a relationship between Robert Mariolle and the Countess Mosska).

The Foreign Soul
[L'Ame étrangère]

I

There were still few people in the gaming room because that evening, for the first time, the theatre of the new Aix casino was staging a comedy by Henry Meilhac.[1] Around the four tables, however, a wreath of regulars—men and women, seated and standing—were already crowding, enclosing the croupiers in the usual circle of tireless gamblers. But the rest of the big room remained empty; empty were the long divans squatting at the foot of the walls, the low armchairs in the corners, the chairs with already tarnished leather. The anterior salon was also deserted, and the doorman walked there, hands behind back, the kindly doorman whose responsibility it was to spot the dubious people seeking to enter this place without having been introduced and stamped as honest by the gambling authorities' visa.[2]

The sound of money, discreet but continuous, the slight noise of the spring of gold, of the spring of louis[3] flowing over the four baizes, was singing beneath the yet more discreet, calm and muffled human voices.

A man came forward to enter, tall, thin, youngish. He had the easy air of bachelors who have spent their adolescence in the elegant habits of a rich and Parisian life. The top of his head was balding, but the remaining blond hair that surrounded it frizzed nicely about his temples, and a pretty moustache, twirled at the ends by a little curling iron, spread out nicely on his top lip. His light blue eyes seemed kindly and cocky, and he carried about his whole person a bold appearance, of affability and gracious disdain, showing that he wasn't a very recent parvenu or one of those casino prowlers who roam the world in search of plunder.

As he went to go through the big opening draped with a hanging door-curtain, the doorman, very politely, approached him, asking:

'Would you remind me of your name monsieur?'

He answered without stopping:

'Robert Mariolle. I was registered this afternoon.'

'Perfect, monsieur, thank you.'

And so he went into the second room, looking around for someone.

A voice called him, and a man of small stature, slightly overweight, pushing forty, perfectly proper, wearing one of those strange first communicant's jackets known as *tuxedos*,[4] made fashionable by partying princes, approached, hands outstretched.

Mariolle took his hands and shook them, a smile upon his lips, saying:

'Hello, mon cher Lucette.'

The Count de Lucette, an amiable, rich, and happy-go-lucky bachelor, spent his days and years going where everyone went, doing what everyone did and saying what everyone said with a certain good-natured spirit which made him sought after. Showing his interest, he asked:

'Well! and the heart?'

'Oh! it's alright, it's over.'

'Entirely?'

'Yes.'

'You've come to Aix to convalesce?'

'Like you said. A change of air.'

'Yes, the air where you have loved can always harbour its dangerous microbe.'

'No, mon cher. There isn't any danger anymore. But I was with her for three years. So I have to change my habits; and for that there's nothing like travelling.'

'You arrived this morning?'

'Yes.'

'And you're going to stay here a while?'

'Until I grow bored.'

'Oh! you won't get bored, it's entertaining here, very entertaining even.'

And Lucette painted a picture of Aix. He recounted this town of showers and casinos, of hygiene and pleasure, where all the princes on earth that have been cast off their thrones fraternized with all the flashy foreigners that the prisons

Chapter One

didn't want. He expressed, with his familiar verve, this unique muddle of socialites and hussies, dining at neighbouring tables, speaking in loud voices about each other, and playing, an hour later, shoulder to shoulder about the same baize. He wittily portrayed this little town of Savoy—the suspect familiarity, this incomprehensible kindness of people unapproachable elsewhere who have chosen to party and get together with any old body. The same highnesses, the same future or deposed sovereigns, dukes, grand dukes or little dukes, uncles, cousins, or stepbrothers of kings, the same French or cosmopolitan grandes dames who ordinarily put immeasurable distances between themselves and the simple bourgeois, who formed, during the winter, in Cannes, impenetrable aristocratic groups that English hypocrisy or immense American and Jewish fortunes can only half-open, these same groups hurry as soon as it gets warmer to the noisy casinos of Aix, their only wish being, it's said, to mix freely with the riffraff.

With the jovial and disdainful tone of a well brought up man showing someone round a bad place, the Count de Lucette recounted how it pleased him, mocking himself as much as others, and exaggerating the picture to make it all the more striking. His little chubby face, clean shaven, which the ends of two sideboards cut neatly to the ears made even broader, had the cheerful lively comical expression, a little put on, of those well-born dilettantes who are witty in salons, and he cited deeds, told anecdotes, named women, exposed with good will scandals of love and gambling.

Mariolle listened to him with a smile on his lips, nodding approval every now and then, with the appearance of finding this well-prepared gossip exquisite, but his blue eyes seemed dulled, veiled by a thought only just chased away.

His friend had finished speaking, there was a silence, and he said, as though he had forgotten Aix and all of those people evoked:

'Do you know the last dirty trick she played me?'

The other, greatly surprised, asked:

'What trick? By whom?'

'Henriette.'

'Ah! formerly your beloved?'

'Yes.'

'No, I don't know. Go on.'

'She got me to lend money to a clothes seller at whose house she had rendezvous.'

Lucette burst out laughing, finding the trick delightful.

Mariolle resumed:

'Yes, she moved me to pity, making out to me this procuress was her cousin. There was the story of a seduction and the abandonment of a child left in the charge of this poor woman; a total fiction, an idiotic fiction, devised in the head of a whore and a concierge's daughter.'[5]

Lucette was still laughing.

'And you were taken in?'

'Well, yes.'

'It's funny, you being who you are, how you were raised, in your dad's lap, old Mariolle, the craftiest of men.'

Mariolle made a little shrug of his shoulders full of disdain for himself and perhaps everyone; and he mumbled:[6]

'With women, the finest are the idiots.'

'Mon cher, when you love them, they generally become bitches.'

'That's perhaps a bit of an exaggeration.'

'No. But when they love, they are angels, angels with claws, vitriol, or anonymous letters, sometimes only clamping angels, but angels of fidelity, self-sacrifice, and devotion... In any case, it's upset you, although your Henriette was, I think, a repeat offender.'

'Yes but her subsequent offences rightly prepared me for the cure, and I am cured of her.'

'Really?'

'Really. Three times is too much.'

'So it's the third time you've caught her out.'

'Yes.'

'When you wrote to me the day before yesterday to book you a room in my hotel, you had just sussed her.'

'Yes.'

'So your discovery is totally recent.'

'Oh yes. Four days ago.'

'Damn! beware of relapses.'

'Oh! no! I vouch for myself.'

And, to make himself feel better, Mariolle told his liaison in its entirety, as if

Chapter One

he wanted to be shot of her, to banish from his mind and his heart this memory, this story and its details from which he was still bruised.

His father, a former député, became a minister, then director of a large politico-financial bank, *the Union of industrial towns*,[7] where he amassed a great fortune, he died leaving his only son an annuity of more than five hundred thousand francs, begging him as some last advice to spend his life doing nothing and making fun of others. He was a wily old bird of finance, sceptical, sly and guilty, who had opened the eyes of his heir at an early age to all the sly tricks of humanity.

At his school, soon initiated into the schemes of money and power junkies, Robert became one of those elegant young men for whom existence, when he had reached thirty years, already seemed to hold no more secrets.

Endowed with a subtle intelligence and a sardonic perspicacity kindled by a sense of natural honesty, he let himself drift in the current of time, avoiding worries and sampling all he found good in his path. Without family, for he had lost his mother a few months after his birth, without keen passions and without irresistible impulses, for a long time he kept his heart free of ties, attracted only by pleasures, the scene and all the delights of Paris, and even more by a certain taste for paintings and objets d'art. This taste had first arisen because one of his friends was a collector, but also because he loved instinctively fine and rare things, and because he had just bought a pretty house on the avenue Montaigne[8] which needed to be furnished and decorated, and finally because he had nothing else to do. A few months and a lot of money was sufficient for him to become what you'd call an enlightened amateur, one of those people who can be well versed in something because they're rich, and who inspire fashionable painters because they pay them. Like so many others, by dint of buying canvases and knick-knacks, he gained the right to have an opinion; he was considered and consulted; he encouraged trends and misjudged talents; he was one of those who each year fill the Palais de l'Industrie with those trashy paintings which are awarded medals through complaisance in order to give them easy passage into the galleries of art lovers.[9]

Then he lost his ardour, having recognized that everyone is mistaken in that as in other things, that nobody knows about anything and that opinions change with fashion, and that that affects aesthetics just as it affects clothes.

Increasingly indifferent and sceptical, like a true Parisian of thirty-five years, he confined himself to the usual pleasures of men on the cusp of becoming bachelors. He reasoned his business, saw clarity in his existence, took the rational into account in each distraction, gambling, horses, theatre, society and the rest.

He fairly loved society, dining with pleasure in town, and then between ten and one in the morning making long visits to favoured salons where he was a regular. He was well received, fêted, cherished because of his wealth, his wit, and a kind of sympathy which he attracted.

A real Frenchman of the old stock, amiable, cheeky, disdainful of everything which didn't rouse him, ignorant of everything which didn't amuse him, only having attention for certain things, certain people, even certain areas of Paris; he considered, on the whole, that existence wasn't worth making a lot of effort for and that it should make you laugh rather than cry.

And so it was that he met at a supper the mistress of one of his friends. She immediately appealed to him with her discreet charm which was more all-pervasive than obvious. On sitting down next to her you barely noticed her; after an hour of talking you felt yourself melted by her grace. She was a pretty, thin woman, in half-tones, of a reserved kind with modest and delicate manners which showed a domesticity in this distinguished demi-monde.

Almost unknown amidst the famous clan of high courtesans, she had always been the accredited mistress of someone, staying in the shadows, the sumptuous and perfumed shadows. She was one of those adroit women who know how to give domestic joys to the single men of the high life, and who maintain, until the naïf lover destined to marry them finds them out, the speciality of making rich idle men pay very dearly for the appearance of a genuine home.

Robert Mariolle fell in love with her, paid court to her as to a society woman, dared declarations, wrote of his affection. Knowing of his wealth, she made him wait a bit, then gave in, settling him into a false adultery just as she had settled her other lover into a false conjugal happiness. When she was certain of his attachment to her, she felt remorse and declared to him that she had to break with one or other of them. If he wanted her, she would be his. He was delighted by this choice and replied that he would take her.

And so very skilfully, without fuss or quarrels, she split from him who paid for her discreet favours. Her life wasn't disrupted by it; the two men weren't even very angry with each other and, after a frostiness of a few weeks in which they kept their distance from each other, they shook hands again and were friends as before.

Chapter One

And so Mariolle had two residences, one of which stashed paintings, rare furniture, bronzes, a thousand expensive objects, whilst the other hid a pretty woman, always ready to receive him, to distract him with smiles, tender words and caresses. He liked her place and little by little spent his idleness there, moving his life there. At first he had the habit of dining there every now and again, then more often, then every night. He received friends there and had little parties where she did the honours with a simple elegance of which he was very proud. Around her he tasted the rare joy of having a kind of slave to love, charming, accommodating, devoted and paid. She held to perfection this role of acting the wife and he was attached so greatly to the happiness she gave him that in the end it had to be unforeseen in flagrante delicto to convince him he was deceived.

A duel took place. He was very lightly wounded and resumed his former life. But after two months of an existence which seemed odious to him, he met Henriette one morning on the street. She came to him, flushed, moved out of audacity and timidity.

'I love you', she said. 'If I have deceived you, it's because I'm a whore [*fille*]. You know that well, besides. By that I mean that I had an impulse. Who doesn't? Were you always faithful to me whilst I was your mistress? Tell me, did you never see again with affection a former girlfriend?—No, don't say anything. I was paid, it's not the same thing.'

The explanation lasted two hours, on the pavement, going up and down one road and another. He showed himself hard, quick-tempered, vehement; she was humble, touching, nervous. She cried, unworried at being in public, without drying her eyes, real tears, for she loved him in her way, this whore [*fille*].

He was moved, consoled her, came to see her the following day, and took her back. 'Bah', he said to absolve himself, 'she's only my mistress, after all.'

However he modified his way of life, no longer opening the door of his mistress to his friends, save a few, one of which was the Count de Lucette, and living with her in a closer but at the same time more reserved manner.

She ended up conquering him through the pleasantness of her intimacy, through her kind attentions, through a certain funny malicious wit that she seemed to save for him, even by the readings she did for him in the evening, when they were alone. He came to prefer a tête-à-tête with her to the majority of distractions which amused him at other times. But one morning a letter discovered in the hands of the chambermaid revealed to him the name of a new rival.

He judged that it would be naïf and ridiculous to fight a second time for this little minx, and he simply left her. Now as he had lived for two years in unceasing contact with that caressing flesh—coupled with nostalgia for established habits, favourite kisses, which he didn't manage to forget or replace with others—it made for three months of troubled nights and anxious days for him.

She wrote to him: he didn't reply. A second letter shook him. She owned up, pleading mitigating circumstances and asking him the favour of coming to see her, just as a friend, from time to time.

He resisted for six weeks then surrendered to her entreaties. A few days later they were living together again.

That lasted for a year, then he received the visit from the old clothes seller who had several times assisted Henriette's solicitations. The two women had fallen out, the old procuress had simply come out of vengeance to reveal that she had lent her house for the rendezvous of her young client.

And so he was completely enraged, so exasperated he felt healed, as if he had a scar upon his heart. He resolved to have nothing more to do with women who liaise with paying masters and who are troubled by nothing and he left Paris for a change of scenery and a change of life.

His thoughts were drawn towards Aix because he could find his friend the Count de Lucette there, and, having joined him, he soon told him this painful story which the other, moreover, almost knew entirely already, from fragments. He listened to him till the end however with a mocking attention, then, looking Mariolle in the eyes:

'When will you take her back?' he said.

'Oh! never.'

'Come on.'

'Never.'

'But, joker, you've been here half an hour and the only thing you've talked about is her.'

'Sorry, I was talking about myself. Everyone does it.'

'Yes, but in regard to her.'

'As I would talk about myself regarding a voyage if I had come back from China or Japan, that wouldn't mean I was going to go back there.'

'It proves that you're thinking of her.'

Chapter One

'Oh! only tonight.'

'Of course, it's a dangerous hour.'

'In the morning, on waking, I was delighted, delighted to the depth of my heart to have broken up. Throughout the day I no longer thought of her, as if she didn't exist; then, when night fell, it brought back memories to me, a few intimate memories that made me slightly melancholy. But I despise her so much that it's completely over.'

They were distracted by the entrance of a crowd. The show had finished; and whilst the public who go to bed early were heading back to their hotels and villas, the public who go to bed late invaded the gaming rooms. Tarts, old tarts of the beaches and casinos, those of Biarritz, Dieppe, and Monte Carlo, the legendary look-outs for players on a roll, the Delabarbe sisters, Rosalie Durdent, the great Marie Bonnefoy, in their hunting dress, all their heads capped by hats standing out like lighthouses above them, they arrived, surrounded by men who, big, little, fat or thin, were wearing, hanging off their bony backs or puffed out by their fat figures, that comical little jacket invented, so it's said, by the future king of England.[10]

Society women also, of the best society, the very grandest society, appeared escorted by a court of gentlemen:[11] the Princess de Guerche, the Marquise Epilati, Lady Wormsbury—the very beautiful Englishwoman, one of the favourite girlfriends of the Prince of Wales, a connoisseur—and her rival, Mrs Filds, the blonde American.

And suddenly, although the sound of footsteps and words grew ceaselessly, the ringing of gold on the tables increased so much that its little metallic voice, continuous and clear, dominated the human noises.

Mariolle now looked about, recognizing faces, and with the pretensions of an expert in feminine beauty, started up with Lucette those discussions that all men of the world have had. A new face appeared, a brunette, brown as they are on the borders of the Orient, having on her brow and temples that thick eruption of black hairs which seem to encircle a woman with the night. Of average height, she had a slender waist, a full bosom, a lithe gait, an air of vivacity and indolence at the same time, and that bearing of aggressive beauty which throws defiance to the looks of all.

'Look out, she's pretty, that one', said Mariolle.

Lucette replied:

'I'll introduce you if you like.'

'Who is she?'

'The Countess Mosska, a Romanian.'

'It's funny', resumed Mariolle, 'I've never really been attracted to brunettes.'

'Come on, why not?'

'I don't know; just haven't. And then I prefer chestnut or blonde hair.'

'Blondes are dyed.'

'Ah no, mon cher.'

'Oh yes, my dear chap, or at least some of them are dyed, and so well dyed that you can't tell them from the real ones, and even the best connoisseurs can be mistaken. They have become rare like authentic trinkets, and you can never be sure what you're embracing.'

'Ah no, no. They have a grace that the brunettes don't possess. The nape of the neck for example. Do you know of anything more pretty in the world than the light frizz of short hairs, the first golden or chestnut hairs with glimmers of mahogany on the white skin of the neck which go down fading away into the shoulders? Brunettes have a hard appearance, they are the warriors of love. Look at that one there. The Amazon of coquetry, you might say. Do you remember the slow gait and tender behaviour of Henriette?'

'Well sure, she was doing her job, she was.'

After a moment of reflection, Mariolle added:

'No matter, if she'd been a little less cheap, or perhaps a little more, we would have formed an inseparable couple.'

Several men had spotted them, advancing with hands outstretched. It was only: 'Hello, Mariolle. — Fancy you're here? — How are you? — When did you arrive? So you've left Paris, have you?'

And Mariolle shook hands, smiling, answering that he was in the best of health, and that he'd come to do a bit of partying at Aix.

Suddenly one of them, a very noble Italian, ruined and a spa town lingerer, the Marquis Pimperani, asked him:

'Do you know the Princess de Guerche?'

'Yes, I hunt and sometimes even dine at her house.'

'Come and say hello to her; she'll invite you to a little trip to the country we're making tomorrow.'

Chapter One

The princess, a thin little woman, almost always dressed in a slightly masculine way, woollen cloth jackets tailored at the waist and dresses of a nimble appearance indicating the woman who walks, who hunts and rides horses, was chatting with Mrs Filds, in the middle of a group of men pressing around them like a defensive escort.

When she noticed Mariolle, she offered him her hand, amicably, saying:

'Well, hello, monsieur. So you're here at Aix.'

She introduced him immediately to the beautiful American whose clear face was always smiling the same smile under a dazzling blaze of blonde hair. It wasn't the vaporous cloud with which certain English faces are haloed, but lustrous sunlit hair, like a ripe harvest from virgin soil. She was famous in all the capital cities.

They chatted. The princess never gambled. She came there to watch as a spectator, for she was taking a serious cure, having suffered rheumatisms from hunting last autumn. From a very good family, and very well bred, she had pushed to the extreme a taste for horses and sports. Nothing but that occupied, interested or fascinated her. Aged about thirty years, not pretty, but pleasant, with a boyish appearance, sweet blue and plucky eyes, pretty chestnut hair, a supple, elegant and muscular thinness, she loved to amuse herself running through woods, killing animals, throwing parties, setting off fireworks, horse riding with men, with no apparent concern for gallantry. Her husband, a député of an arrondissement of Touraine where he owned a magnificent residence, gave her great freedom and concerned himself almost exclusively with historic researches.

He had already received two prizes from the Académie française.[12] His library of manuscripts was held up as an example throughout the knowledgeable European world.

The princess asked Mariolle:

'Have you come out of pain?'

'No, princess.'

'So it's for amusement?'

'Oh yes, quite simply.'

'That couldn't be better. So do you want to come on our trip tomorrow to Chambotte?'[13]

'Gladly.'

'Great! we meet at ten, after the cure, in front of the Hôtel des Souverains.'[14]

He thanked her, delighted by the invitation which gave him more intimate entry into a world which he had still yet to penetrate.

The little Marquise Epilati, then the tall Lady Wormsbury, a *professional beauty*,[15] who were prowling around the gaming tables, risking a few louis from time to time from the hand of a friend, drew nearer and sat down. And they both busied themselves with the people that were swarming around them, chiefly whores [*filles*]. The men were mentioning names, giving detailed accounts in hushed voices, whispering scabrous particulars. A story about Rosalie Durdent greatly amused them, and the last adventure of the older of the Delabarbe sisters, who had arrived at the hotel the evening before, really seemed a bit too vivid, although the Count de Lucette told it admirably.

But the princess, thinking of her health, suddenly said:

'It's getting late. Let's go and have our cup of tea. Then we'll return.'

She got up, followed by her entire group and they went off through the long glass gallery between two parks adorned by jets of water during the day and artificial fires in the evening, it was an immense café, a dining room where those bored by the table d'hôte of the hotels and who had a profusion of money lunched and dined.

There, suddenly, around cups of steaming tea, a new conversation began, completely different, familiar, mondaine, in another tone, a kind of exchange of broken, habitual chatter, always renewed, which, between these women of diverse origins and these men of such disparate races, seemed to show the strange freemasonry of a unique and borderless upper class. About them the crowd passed, swarming, the vulgar crowd, banal, bustling, the crowd of humble and common, even rich and well-known, people. They were no longer there, for them! They were no longer interested in them, could no longer see the crowd. They had just broken off from it, unostentatiously parted from it to regroup themselves around a coffee table as they would do in a princely salon.

Presently they spoke amongst themselves of people of their class, not those present, but absentees, French, Russian, Italian, English, German, who they seemed to know like brothers, like neighbours, for all the names mentioned, which for the most part Mariolle was ignorant of, seemed familiar to all their ears.

Slightly disorientated in their midst, all of a sudden mixing with this small borderless aristocratic population, he listened with curiosity to this international

Chapter One

elite of the *high life* [16] which knew, recognized and met up with each other everywhere, in Paris, Cannes, London, Vienna, or St Petersburg, a caste established through birth, education, a tradition of chic, the same notion of distinguished life, and also through marriage, consecrated above all through relations at court and royal friendships which raise them almost above the popular and banal prejudice of nationalities.

Only the slight accent of origin which stamped all these mouths revealed that the language they used—depending on the towns where they found themselves—wasn't their mother tongue.

The princess and Mariolle, sitting beside her, soon split off from the others into a private discussion. To please her he spoke in praise of her hunts, her remarkable talent as a horsewoman, her ardour in following the hounds. Carried away by her passion she already showed in her eyes and her voice that special kindness of people who have their quirks pandered to; then they discussed travels, the sea, mountains, the Alps. Aix's surroundings provided a good source of stories.

'The trip we're going to take tomorrow,' she said, 'is a marvellous one. I won't describe it to you, as you're going to see it.'

Then to prove to him that he had just gained her friendship:

'Hey, I'll take you in my carriage with a charming little woman, the Countess Mosska, a Romanian.'

He asked:

'She was just now in the gaming room, wasn't she?'

'Yes, with her father, the old man with a white moustache and goatee.'

And so the princess provided a few details about this young woman whose beauty was causing a sensation in Aix. She was the widow of Count Mosska, the king's equerry, killed in a duel following a gambling quarrel. The accident was barely eighteen months ago, since then she had travelled, having left Bucharest to get over, it was said, her profound grief.

'And she is better?' enquired Mariolle with an imperceptible nuance of irony.

The princess smiled, replying:

'I think so.'

Then she got up, for she had a routine imposed by the regimen of the waters and, when she had left, Mariolle, in his turn, headed off, wanting to make a tour of the park before going to bed.

This hour spent with these elegant women, contact with whom was sweet, had animated, cheered him up and consoled him. He felt, without a doubt, that his remaining melancholy had vanished in the midst of these people who welcomed him favourably, and he started to think of them as one does on leaving very interesting and unfamiliar beings.

He walked for a long time in the pathways of the park, beneath the hot night, the stifling night of this little town at the bottom of a valley, which was like a steam room in the summer months; but as the direct sensation of the women he'd just left slipped away from him, the impression of solitude, that had returned every evening since his split from Henriette, invaded him anew. The shadows seemed boundless to him and the earth empty, for no longer would anyone be waiting for him in his room at bedtime. As he had said to the Count de Lucette, there is the joy of the morning, that kind of indeterminate hope which awakens in our heart, each day as we do; then the disturbances of life and its contacts, its habitual little distractions, parted him until evening from the undefined need for tenderness and the definite need for caresses, that had now entered him, as happens to all those who have lived for a long time in an amorous intimacy. The crisis returned at the same time, bringing memories and desires with which were mixed rancour, a renewed anger towards this little minx from whom he had suffered, and suffered still. He congratulated himself however on finally having dropped her, and as though to affirm, console and convince himself that he wouldn't regret it, he repeated to himself: 'Crikey, what luck that it's over!'

He went back very slowly, reached his room, went to bed, and, as he was tired out from his journey and his day, he fell asleep almost straight away.

II

Robert Mariolle was awoken early by the sound of movement in the hotel. Through the panes of his window, the awning of which he hadn't closed, a flood of sunlight lit up the walls and white curtains of his room, a little pool of light so vivid that he couldn't stay in bed.

Soon up, he left and headed off following the narrow corridor whose doors seemed to be guarded by shoes, ankle boots and boots that had just been shined. These pieces of delicate or sturdy leather spoke of the life, customs, elegance and the social condition of those still in bed behind the walls. Mariolle thought about it, smiling, full of the morning's good humour, wanting to try and gain entry when he saw on their own the fine shoes of two petite feet, or full of disdain for the sturdy hobnailed soles of tourists from which he could detect snoring in passing. Suddenly, he noticed, completely blocking the way, a kind of chest shrouded by curtains, and which two huffing Savoyards were carrying. At first glance it gave the impression of an accident, the slight pang of anguish caused by the covered stretcher encountered on the street, then he remembered he was in a mineral spa town, where the patients in treatment are removed from their beds and taken back to them after the showers. On the staircase he had to stop two more times to let pass these sedan chairs [1] and he realized where they were coming from.

....
....

VARIANT

'With women, the finest are the idiots.'
'When you love them.'
'I never loved her.'
'Henriette Lambel?'
'Yes, Henriette Lambel, I never loved her.'
'Say that again?'
'I never loved her.'
'No... that's too much, that is.'
'It's the truth, mon cher.'
'Ah, so why have you been clinging to her for three years whilst she's been a bitch? For you know that, that she's been a bitch.'
'I know it.'
'She's deceived you. Did you know that she deceived you?'
'I knew.'
'So you accepted everything, which is excusable when you're in love, but which becomes incomprehensible when you're not in love.'
'Mon cher, listen. I'm going to try and make you understand me, which won't be easy, and to explain to you the type of attachment which tied me to that whore [*fille*].'
'Oh! I guess: the body and its wiles.'
'No, something else: her perverse charm.'
'So, you loved her?'

'No, I suffered an attraction which I detested, against which I couldn't defend myself.'

'That's one of the forms of love.'

'No, it's one of the forms of human weakness, and one of the proofs of the power and the danger of education.'

'What are you on about now?'

'Listen, you know me well enough to understand me, since we've been friends from college. You spoke to me just now about dad. You remember what kind of man he was, the craftiest sceptic that I've known, a fat, jovial sceptic, without pessimism, as they say today, a sceptic who was twice minister in an age where one really saw some funny things. And he saw them very well, scented them, guessed them, uncovered them with his calm cunning and radical unbelief. Under my father's tutelage, I learnt human beastliness as you naturally learn to swim when you are thrown in the water every day. I didn't ignore that it was beastliness and that you drown in it, but I kept a certain blameworthy fondness for it; and moreover I know how to swim. So I lived in this extraordinarily rotten world which meddled with governments, in the midst of men who do all sorts; married women who are whores [*filles*] and whores [*filles*] that I could, in my soul and conscience, no longer distinguish from the married women. Brought up in that world, I loved it, as men who grow up in the fields love the plains, as men who grow up in the towns love the streets. I really love that, that an honest woman, but just that, a really honest woman, bores me as much as a rural clergyman, even if she is extremely beautiful. As for those who aren't honest, they please me, but I despise them, yes, mon cher, I despise them in the name of a certain honesty that I have but don't make use of openly, or, rather, of which I make use solely to make judgments that I put away in my private files. I despise lots of people in this way, lots of things, lots of ideas which I have the appearance of making my delights, for I am tolerant and conciliatory, good-natured and sometimes abrupt, when it pleases me to be abrupt, through caprice. Now, you knew Henriette Lambel. That woman was just made to delight me at first sight. It's by her felinity and her perfidy that she seduced me. In her I found, I recognized, I savoured all the loathsome faults of women. And then there was such an irresistible and incomprehensible harmony between her delicious person and her execrable nature, that it might've sufficed to do the corrupt person that I am up like a kipper. Is she pretty, the wench, with her discreet movements, with that finesse of features, of look, smile, skin, limbs, fingers, which give her a unique savour?! She is without any doubt the most gracious creature that I have known. And with that, with that gentle appearance, loving, faithful, devoted, she lies as nobody has ever lied, she lies with the authority of a fencing master striking his pupils where he wants. I was forewarned, I was ignorant of nothing, and I was taken in completely by her lies. God! what a bitch!'

He recounted his passion, his heart was still completely full of this subject. He spoke of the beginning, disguising his naïf impulse under an air of sceptical bravado, not admitting that he had been in love, blind and silly like all those who fall into the hands of a woman whose profession is to play with men.

With his casual, indifferent, ironic tones, he presently made fun of himself. After having recognized his weakness and discovered all the tricks, all the ruses of which he had been a victim. After having truly sounded out the perfidious heart of woman to its falsest corners, he posed as a man who hadn't been duped, but had closed his eyes through disdain and amusement.

He had closed his eyes, and often. He had first closed them on meeting her for the first time. She was a courtesan of semi-greatness, already rich, though very young, endowed with the suppleness and instinct of irresistible girls [fille]. Tall, thin, slim, seductive, feline, she didn't have the glamour that made men turn around in the street, but a veiled attraction, almost modest, an ingratiating seduction of voice, smile, and gesture, with which she ensnared all those who had crossed her door.

Mariolle, for six months, thought himself loved by her, and he loved her simply, the good boy, in spite of his pretensions of cunning. Then, a little detail, all of a sudden, opened his eyes. He learnt through his friends' stockbroker that Henriette Lambel had just invested one hundred thousand francs in railway bonds.

Where did she get these one hundred thousand francs?

He reasoned, spied, sought and realized that he had been deceived. At first he wanted to fight, to kill someone, and he called, as seconds, two friends. His two seconds revealed to him that he would find ahead of him four adversaries at least. Four were named. Perhaps there were even more. He had an impulse of pride and broke with her, after an abominable scene.

Then he regretted it, he suffered, he cried.

They went back to the house where they met up, an actress's place, at first they spoke to each other haughtily, then with kindness, then with gentleness, then tenderness. She took him back swearing to be faithful to him, and, in return for an allowance judged sufficient for the needs of a pretty woman, he kept all the keys to the apartment.

That lasted six months. He saw nothing suspect, living, however, prey to all suspicions. But one morning a letter discovered in the hands of the chambermaid revealed to him once more that he wasn't alone. The argument was terrible. He beat his mistress, then split from her again. But during this second period of their liaison, more ardent and less trusting than the first, he had become attached to her in a strange and stubborn way, not to the being that he had believed sincere, but to the being which he knew was deceitful. He loved this woman with an irritable love, exciting and jealous, he loved her like we love whores [*filles*] who overexcite our desires when we make them our regular companions because they are public creatures who we feel are always ready to slide into the arms of another.

So, after a separation of six weeks, he returned to her and took back the keys, knowing well that they were duplicates. He closed his eyes readily, and as she had the control, a lot of skill and tact, she knew how to handle his self-esteem. But, noting her power over him, she became one of those very capricious rulers and made existence intolerably enervating for him. She imposed her mother, the widow of a carter, on him at dinner, and going to see her little sister in boarding school at Sèvres; and she swiped money from him under all imaginable pretexts.

These vexations had a greater influence on him than her infidelities. He had his eyes open upon her, lucid and scornful eyes, and all the while tasting the physical charm, perverse and appetizing, of this refined courtesan, he learnt through her to know, discern and hate all feminine duplicities. He observed her with avid curiosity, and kept a check on himself with a flattering complacency. Posing as a strong, sceptical and corrupt man, who rationalized his passions, giving into them or analysing them, according to the current fashion, he claimed to know himself admirably, and to never ignore the dictates of the motives he followed be they instinctive or intentional.

So he kept a check on himself methodically, believing he was absolutely clearheaded and talked about himself with the petty pride of a very gifted man who is fully aware of his qualities; of course he judged as it pleased him to judge, amplifying, according to his vanity, what he was anxious to show, concealing what he was anxious to hide, seeing big with myopic eyes his favourite flaws and merits alike, for anyone who looks at himself is too close to the subject to perceive clearly.

This practice of observation saved him, however, from the domination of Henriette. He was bad at guessing her wily tricks, but discovered them in the end and above all he got angry at the childish traps she constantly set about him. The pointless caprices, the bellicose coquetry, the need she experienced to frustrate him because she was the strongest, gradually fermented in the lucid soul of this man an accumulated, disguised, growing rancour which became an irritation, then a sort of lover's hatred, in spite of his masculine affection; he was always seduced, but disgusted, exasperated and ready to snap from the first day.

When he discovered that, through an odious perversity of humour, she had got him to give money to the procuress whose lodgings had been used for her rendezvous, he was angry, finally, in a definitive way and, very resolutely, split from her forever.

Now it was over, completely over. He was certain he wouldn't take her back. But he was still shaking himself out of it, he was shaking off not the remaining affection, rather remaining habits.

François Tassart's account of research for *The Foreign Soul*[1]

July 3, we're at Aix-les-Bains. My master installs us in a lodge belonging to the *Hôtel de l'Europe*.[2] This pretty den is on an out of the way path on the hillside which rises in the direction of le Revard.[3] The view there is beautiful; the Dent du Chat which overlooks the chain of mountains skirting the south-west part of the lac du Bourget is directly opposite.[4] M. de Maupassant takes his meals at the hotel since he hasn't come here to write but to glean notes with *The Foreign Soul* in mind.

He goes to the *Villa des Fleurs*[5] several times during the day; he follows closely everywhere, as far as it's possible, a Russian princess who lives in the lodge occupied in bygone days by the Empress Eugénie...[6]

One day he appointed me for the evening 'to go to his seedbed of human flowers', as he called it, and he showed me the lady in question... After having lost two louis at petits chevaux,[7] I retired and went to the barrel of the lake which reflected the moon endlessly in its surface.

I followed for a long time the snaking lawn which is shaped by the winding outline of the lake's edge; in the calm depth of the night, I heard the water of the springs running, babbling as they fell. What a pretty memory I have kept of that evening! The beautiful light, the great calm, the light sound of the water, the gentle balminess and the nice scent of the grass which the sun had heated throughout the day! I would gladly have slept under the beautiful starlight, especially if I had had access to a boat on which I would have let myself be lulled on the water so clear and limpid. But there's more to it than just dreaming, my master should have returned: I hastened back to our lodge.

The following day at the servants' lunch, thanks to a few words of Russian, I struck up the acquaintance of the valet of the princess. The day before we had pushed billiard balls around on the green baize at the café, and, the following day, at 4 o' clock in the afternoon, I had an exquisite Russian cream tea in the salon of Her Highness's lady's companion. Two days later we went together to the théâtre du Cercle.

Now I could furnish my master with the information that he ardently desired on this exotic personality and he knew how to take marvellous advantage of it.

Our princess had her position marked out for a good part in *The Foreign Soul*. I never understood just how Monsieur thought of interpreting this lady's situation in his novel. What I can say, besides a thousand interesting little details about the life of this princess, is there was one thing that struck me which is that she had two lovers who never quit her and who, like two docile and much-loved youngest sons, slept in two little beds placed either side of that of Her Highness. The prince-husband was, it seems, a very highly placed government official who only came rarely to France, just when his duty called for it.

One afternoon, it was so hot that I abandoned going for a walk. I returned to the chalet, the bearer of a tub of grapes, for here M. de Maupassant always followed, at the same time as his series of showers, a cure of white grapes. He hears me return and calls me. I showed him the box of fruits which he found to his taste and placed on the table beside his bed. Then he says to me: 'Because of this intolerable heat, I thought that it would be imprudent to go for a walk. Also I am stretched out on my bed, and, for once in your life you don't have too much work, so try also to rest. Here, in this backwater, we lack air...'

All the while eating grapes, he began to tell me his *Foreign Soul*. But I was really overwhelmed by the heat in this room, so I couldn't remember what he said to me. Seeing me suffocated by the temperature, he authorized me to open the North-facing window a bit and the salon door. This revived me a little; Monsieur laughed whilst nibbling his grapes.

Then he says to me: 'What I'm now going to tell you isn't from the novel, but for real. Well! here it is: M. X... at his place has added to his wife a really beautiful young Greek woman, my word, almost of pure stock. Her ingenuousness, her naïveté, her youth, have knocked me off my stride a little up until now; but I don't believe the moment is far off when I will overcome this obstacle. It would be really unfortunate to let this old... it would be an unspeakably low act... a crime of lèse-amour!...'[8]

He starts to laugh heartily... and, coming back to the great heat which was making us uncomfortable: 'If it continues', he added, 'I'm going to send word to Bernard and Raymond[9] and we will leave to take to the sea as soon as possible. Underneath the sail we'll always be better. I'll inform you in time. But, tell me, if, by chance, you see an accident, some crime, or even something involving a man's death, a violent death, come and tell me at once, for I would like to take a few notes on this subject.'

Two or three days afterwards, I was coming back from a walk on the road to Marlioz,[10] when I saw behind a bush a man's body hanging from the branch of a tree. I said to myself 'this is the thing for my master.' But straightaway two policemen arrived, followed by a woman; they cut the rope, the subject was already dead, though still warm...

Nevertheless I left at a gymnastic pace to inform my master. But I had a disappointment; he said to me it had to be a violent death by a gun or knife, or a beating with blood, etc. ...

Several times we climbed the Revard. My master stares for a long time, with great attention, at all these mountains and this countryside which surrounds Aix-les-Bains. On one day we stayed up there until night. Monsieur wants to take in the smallest nuances of this entire vast panorama that we have opposite us, coming to light in a beautiful sunset. He is happy, he finds the scene perfect: the sun disappeared in a valley to the right, still lighting up the whole length of the lake and giving its water the tint of a superb fire; the high summits of the mountains are now in the shade. It's the night arriving.

As we descend, my master says to me: 'Did you see clearly? Well, all that, you will find in my novel. Aix and its surroundings will give me a marvellous setting in which to move my characters. I am satisfied. That was beautiful, and I feel that everything I have seen has been truly imprinted in there.' Saying this he touched his forehead.

July 22.—My master seems cheerful today, and, between two smiles which spoke volumes, he announces to me that we are leaving for Cannes the day after tomorrow by the evening train to avoid the heat of the day: 'We'll go *via* Valence; I thought a lot about the Alpine railway through Grenoble,[11] but you have to take slow trains almost the whole way, and that would be more tiring. I now have all my documents, my characters are each rightly in their place; there is nothing more to come back to here, I can see the matter very clearly, absolutely plainly.'

François Tassart's account of Alexandre Dumas fils' involvement with *The Foreign Soul* [1]

It was that day, at table, that, on Mme Pasca's [2] discreet invitation, M. de Maupassant analysed the plan of *The Foreign Soul*, one of his future novels. When he had finished, M. Dumas [3] asked him if he'd like, for a few moments, to admit him as a collaborator.

'Very gladly!' he answered.

M. Dumas unfurled his outlook with regard to the analysis already made, then he started up a discussion which ended with the two parties coming to agreement; but this understanding wasn't realized without lots of jests, witticisms, ripostes, and lively and brilliant sparks which flew out of these two brains, like two electric currents in action.

Mme L... then said: 'My friends, you have just made a very good canvas'. Mme Pasca added: 'And I hope, M. de Maupassant, that it will be finely embroidered.'

'Yes, Madame, I will cover it with those fine silks from the Orient that spiders weave, and from which Aristotle wore the first coat.' [4]

'Perfect', replied Mme Pasca, 'since it concerns the inner feelings of those countries, but I ask you, my friend, if you can grant a favour to an old artist, and this would be of only strewing here and there, in this work, a patch, a miniscule fragment of their flavour.'

That day was one of Mme Pasca's best. Often, during our days of misfortune, she reminded me of it with bitter tears running from her black eyes, for she loved M. de Maupassant as if he had been her child.

This friendship, where literature played its part, had been born in bygone days, in the company of George Sand,[5] at Flaubert's. She made it a point of honour to continue, around little Guy, the friendship he had lost with the death of his literary father, the author of *Madame Bovary*, and which he venerated in all that he said and thought until his final end.[6]

***

Now I would like to place here the adventure that M. Dumas fils told, which helped him subsequently to set up the canvas of *The Foreign Soul*. But my pen trembles, feeling that it will only be able partly to recall the expressions of this fine well-read man. In the heat of the discussion, M. Dumas said:

'My friend, of these beings who place love with its infinite complexities above everything, I can speak with full knowledge of the facts.

'Here we go: So I was twenty-five years old; we were at the dawn of 1850; the revolution had, fortunately, closed its doors, and the official balls had reopened theirs.[7] During one of these soirées, it was given me to see a tall, beautiful, brown woman with satin skin, a dream in full bloom; and the look of her brown eyes, deep and ardent, resembled flaming torches lighting up some Athenian spirit. She threw me into turmoil, and I experienced the strongest sensation of my life with regard to women. After having obtained the favour of a waltz from this lady, during which I was intoxicated by her breath, by the delicious perfume of her flesh, and during which our two svelte bodies were electrified by the contact of one against the other, like two burning sources attracted to each other and striving to get closer, I swept her away towards a lounge room, to a sofa that was screened delightfully by a cluster of palm trees; in this more restrained atmosphere, I said to this lady that I wanted to be her companion, I said all that an enamoured heart can say, all that the heart of a lover can overflow with from love at first sight.

'All the while I was throwing at her feet all the entreaties that my love had suggested to me to awaken in her an echo of the feeling that she had inspired in me, she maintained a cold, impassive calm; not a muscle of her physiognomy relaxed, and my tight, dried out throat seemed to me to be a prelude of a complete failure. Finally, with her left hand she raised her lace scarf, twirling it round a slender palm leaf which was draped over her shoulder. And, with her right hand, pointing out a painting by Drolling, *Jésus discutant devant les docteurs* [Jesus arguing in front of the Doctors],[8] she pronounced: "Yes! my friend, but will you always remind yourself that it's in the presence of the Man-God that you have made your promises?... ".

'This union so hurriedly sealed gave in friendship, in love, all one could dream of it. Sometimes, after passionate transports which have called on all our strength, we fall exhausted.

'... In these moments, where time seemed to have stopped, my thoughts often drifted towards my forebears.

'... For several months our romance slipped by like this, like a dreamland, when, one day, my girlfriend gave me a dispatch from her husband to read which summoned her to return, I raced to the signature: X..., *minister of*... I jumped, my lady friend generously reassured me, saying: "Calm down, my pet, for as to a husband's invitation, there's no hurry to comply".

'But, alas! a day came, for everything must end, when it was the French minister who directed her to return to the head of the marital home. No longer able to turn away from each other for any length of time, our two souls in the same body, so much were they united, the one stuck tight to the other, we travelled by carriage and by boat, always with the same assurance, the same faith, in keeping the promise which tied us together forever. And we still hoped, carried away by our dream in the ethereal spheres, that an unforeseen incident would allow us to live forever united in our happiness. But arriving at the border of the country where her husband was minister, a stoppage took place, and, oh! surprise! two gentlemen surrounded my girlfriend with all the ceremony and consideration due to her rank. As for me, two policemen beseeched me to follow them and we travelled in a special train as far as the port of X..., where they boarded me for le Havre'.[9]

At this moment I served a second dish of calf sweetbreads to M. Dumas: 'They are so light!' — and Mme L... put up her hand: 'Same here, they're so good! they slip across your palate and fill your mouth with flavour as if you were savouring Ostend oysters covered in flavourings from the gardens of Nazareth...'.[10]

Then addressing himself to M. de Maupassant, the unfortunate traveller resumed:

'My friend, when, a good number of years later, I read your masterpiece, *Au Bord de l'Eau*,[11] the memory of our romance was there, alive, like how we lived it at the time. And I remained under the influence of a neurosis which seized me and burnt my entire being to its most intimate depths. With all my soul I cursed this husband who, with no notion of the laws which govern the heart of woman, had shut away this treasure trove of all the graces in a convent, I see it in my mind, this beloved angel, and her profound expression on the day of our union, nowadays entirely colourless spending her time between the bars of her bedroom window, searching for a diversion from her mortal boredom.

'Then I recognized the share of responsibility incumbent upon me for the torments of this captivity, my heart, as much as possible, shared the pain of that which it had loved so much, addressing to it the most sincere regrets as the little it could do to soften her sufferings, and, slowly, I cried as if those tears might have been a caress that I was sending to my girlfriend!'.

Mme L... then said: 'I believe that the marriage blessing has the gift of making husbands jealous; it's true, there are some cuckolds!' [12]

'Even so, if I have the pleasure of knowing the name of the one who pulled this nasty stunt on both of you, I will classify him in the heading of my future novel, *Les Maris Ombrageux* [Touchy Husbands].' [13] 'Oh!' replied Dumas, 'the enigma is very easy to unravel, you only have to find the name of the cavalry general who, during the war of 1855, [14] being unable to get his foot in one of his double boots, [15] turned it over to remove the obstacle that was obstructing it, and, to his great surprise, out popped a magnificent mother hedgehog with all of her young. This general was the brother of the hero of my story. And this surprising find which could have pricked the extremities of the general and made him botch a victory made everyone laugh'.

M. de Maupassant said: 'This mammal would have done better to come in my garden and eat the slugs than to go poisoning itself on exotic perfumes'. [16]

Paul Bourget 'An Unfinished Novel by Maupassant'[1]

I

The Foreign Soul—that's the title of a posthumous fragment of Guy de Maupassant that has just been published—twenty pages of the beginning of an unfinished novel, barely an exposition. And these twenty pages suffice to give the reader an intense sensation of reality, the frisson of life that was the incomparable gift of an unfortunate and great writer... The rooms of a spa town casino, that of Aix, in Savoy, evoke themselves in front of you, and you see the four gaming tables, you hear the sound of louis, 'the slight noise of the spring of gold, of the spring of louis rolling over the four baizes.'[2] Two Parisians are chatting to each other. They haven't exchanged twenty rejoinders yet you already know their characters. One of them is telling his story, a liaison in the demi-monde, a break-up—and all the savour of his passion, that sweetness and bitterness special to each love is made perceptible to you. A crowd begins to flock about and you rub shoulders with them. Some women come into the casino, grandes dames of all countries, an American woman, an Italian marquise, an Englishwoman, a Romanian woman. A few words and you know them, I was going to say that you recognize them all. The cosmopolitan world appears to you in all its complexity, at the same time banal and exceptional, aristocratic and shady, picturesque and monotonous. These women look at you with the blue eyes of the North, in which all the coldness of a misty sky seems to have seeped through; the black eyes of the Midi, burning with sun; eyes of the Orient, velvety and impenetrable. Smiles tremble on fine or sensual lips. You hear breaths, voices; you guess at habits, customs, hard-heartedness, tenderness... A drama of passion is going to get underway... And then nothing! Destiny made the pen fall from the hands of the novelist: the piece that begins like a masterpiece stops abruptly.

II

You close this issue of the review,[3] and sadness seizes hold of your heart—the same sadness which takes a hold of you in Italy on seeing upon the chipped and flaking wall of an old cloister a dying fresco, and the dream of beauty entertained by the artist passing away, devoured by time. Yet the Benozzo Gozzoli of Campo Santo in Pisa, the Ghirlandajo of Santa Maria Novella, the Léonard of Milan,[4] they at least had had the joy of their dreams being realized. The forms which had been living in their minds had taken shape in front of their eyes. If they were dead, it was after having lived a full life, after having enchanted the minds of their creators and communicated the infectiousness of their ideals to thousands of pilgrims. But to have had such forms in your mind's eye and not been able to evoke them, to have felt that they were being carried off into the great night with yourself and that never, never would they reveal themselves outside of you, that is an intellectual agony on top of any physical agony. But it was just that that Maupassant went through, if it's true that in the wretchedness of his last year he ceaselessly asked after a manuscript that he believed had been stolen[5]—either this one [*The Foreign Soul*] or the other, *The Angelus*, likewise unfinished, and which the same review informs us will be published in the next issue.[6] What's a real novel besides a dreamt one and, what's more moving still, that there should be such impotence in such potential, a sudden breaking of shadow over visions that are obliterated, becoming blurred, being destroyed in a mind now incapable of creating them anew! They are, however, within him, and he feels them within, he pursues them, calls them, but cannot find them, and so it was that this soul, at the same time demented and lucid, was invaded with a desperation about which one dare not think.

III

I wrote the word lucid which seems so strange applied to this doubly tragic ending. That is that, in effect, added to the melancholy of an interrupted work—

for those who have a memory of the young Maupassant, heroic in strength and ardour, in health and reason—is the evidence that on the very brink of the crisis into which he sunk, his artistic intelligence remained as sound, as robust and as well-balanced as in the period when he wrote in *les Soirées de Médan* that *Boule de Suif* which placed him as a result amongst the masters.[7] All the powers of the mind that distinguish the storyteller are there intact in their intensity, and this review booklet would suffice to characterize his art. Read it and reread it. You will immediately find within the gift of the *clear compressed turn of phrase*, that power to gather up in a few lines an entire individuality, through an adjective, through the notation of a gesture, a snatch of dialogue. Whilst pages of analysis are necessary for others, even for the greats, for Balzac even, to situate their characters, two phrases are sufficient for Maupassant, as for the two artists whom he resembled the most, Mérimée and Turgenev.[8] I remember having heard the latter, at the table of M. Taine, answer a question from the author of *l'Intelligence*,[9] who asked him:

'But in short, what is, according to you, the premier quality of a novelist?...'

'The gift of painting physiognomies,' said the subtle Russian giant, after having reflected for a minute.

Now take *The Foreign Soul* and look at this physiognomy in the third paragraph: '...A man came forward to enter, tall, thin, youngish. He had the easy air of bachelors who have spent their adolescence in the elegant habits of a rich and Parisian life. The top of his head was balding, but the remaining blond hair that surrounded it frizzed nicely about his temples, and a pretty moustache, twirled at the ends by a little curling iron, spread out nicely on his top lip. *His light blue eyes seemed kindly and cocky, and he carried about his whole person a bold appearance, of affability and gracious disdain...*'[10]—Does that not sufficiently show in a few touches the irreducible individuality of this man's face? The writer hasn't needed technical or new words. The terms that he employs are those that you use yourself every day, but applied with such accuracy that they immediately recapture the full value of their picturesqueness. It was the method of the greatest painter of physiognomies France has had—La Bruyère—, it was that of Stendhal,[11] of Mérimée and Flaubert. It's a greatly superior method to that of the picturesque word in that it augments in a unique way one of the novelist's other essential powers, and one which Maupassant possessed to an unequalled degree: *credibility*.

IV

In this mutilated chapter of *The Foreign Soul*, you experience, in effect, from start to finish, an almost indefinable magic: you can confirm that the old adage about the novelist becoming the historian is true. You accept that the characters he presents to you really exist along with the themes he sets out for you. You can be in no doubt. If you analyse this first chapter, you will perhaps understand more clearly than from reading an entire volume by what methods Maupassant apprehends this ability. You immediately observe his total effacement before the object, his effort to conceal his person from it. Flaubert, who was his great teacher, had formulated this aesthetic rule of the novel in a striking passage: 'The author in his work must be like God in the universe, present everywhere and visible nowhere. Art being a second nature, the creator of this nature must act using analogous methods—so that in all the atoms, in all the aspects is felt an infinite, hidden impassivity...'[12] But to put this, in appearance very simple, rule into practice, you need to take into account what qualities of intelligence, sensibility and conscience are needed: the lofty modesty of the writer who prefers his work to his person, that honesty of spirit which considers talent an instrument of truth and not a tool of vanity—the exactness of the same spirit which discerns in human life profound traits, what M. Taine precisely termed *génératrices* [13]—the exactness of expression also, for an overburdening in expression makes the author show through, the pen too adroit, too ingenious, dispels the enchantment. Finally there must be the power of perspective, this sense of precision which allows the observer to classify each individual encountered in their place in the vast series of social species, without dupery and without disdain. It's with the first of these two faults that writers hypnotized, for example, by the high life, err. With the second fail those who get sick of what they paint. There is in every living being a legitimacy, since they live, and a limitation, since it is only a moment in this vast human universe which is enclosed and passed by on all sides. None of our contemporaries have recognized and demonstrated this near contradictory condition of all existence as Maupassant did. You will see further proof herein in the way in which he portrays the young man who will evidently go on to be the hero of his book. He is, if I'm permitted to say so, an accommodatingly proportioned character,[14] neither too high, nor too low, neither too exceptional, nor too inferior—and because of this the piece soon tackles humanity's compelling value.

There is another value—which increasingly belonged to the writer, as his experience of human life and passions enriched and amplified his technique. Maupassant, especially since *Pierre et Jean*,[15] had come to understand and practise this other law so little known in the art of the novel, and which one cannot grow weary of pointing out: the importance of subject. Nowhere was this preoccupation more manifest than in the last of the works he published: *Notre coeur*.[16] In this book of poignant tone, he had enlarged the anecdote until he made a symbol of it, and, beneath a fairly vulgar salon drama, released one of those sweeping emotional themes, one of those great moral phenomena that interest all hearts. The profound suffering of loving more than one is loved is the intimate subject matter of this novel. An analogous symbolism has to be divined behind the novels. The story told by the author must be able to adapt itself to other events, without the soul with which it has been strongly expressed being changed. If *Pêcheurs d'Islande*, by Loti,[17] is so beautiful it's because it has this charm of representing to a very high-pitched degree the pain of absence. Every man who has suffered from separation finds again his pain in it. Those are great subjects and great books. From nothing more than this title: *The Foreign Soul*, and nothing more than this first chapter, we guess that Maupassant wanted to show that there is something painfully insurmountable in the clash of the races[18]—two beings thrown headlong towards one another by all the frenzies of passion. Seizing each other, desiring each other, loving each other—but always present between them, always alive, this implacable force of heredity which means that the same words spoken by two mouths in the act of feeling their way towards one another do not have the same meaning, and that an invincible misunderstanding always separates a man and a woman coming from two extremes of the historical and physiological world. This would have been—in the form of a love poem, like *Notre coeur*, and as a novel of morals, like *Mont-Oriol*[19]—one of the episodes in the clash of the races that remains one of the least studied and most essential factors of our modern society. And underneath this social symbolism, another would doubtlessly have been hidden: one has heard pass through these pages the profound plaint of the eternal discord and torture, and even in the most complete and tender communion of hearts, they, not being one sole heart, remain irreparably and immortally two.

V

But what's the good of imagining what this book would have been, [this book] by a continually progressing artist to whom success—the worst of ordeals and disastrous to so many others—had been an opportunity only to develop his nature on a higher level?... In carrying out a pious duty for a companion no longer with us, I say again what a powerful and delicate worker of beauty he remained until the end, I cannot prevent myself from addressing a question to the people who are charged with collecting a subscription to raise a monument to this remarkable writer. I remember having read in the *Journal*, a few weeks ago now, a very eloquent article by M. Henri Lavedan,[20] who deplored with justified anger the shortcomings of this subscription. Is that still the case today, after this hearty appeal?* If so, I won't hesitate to say and to say again that it's a shame that our country doesn't better know how to recognize the genius of its great writers. We have let Balzac's manuscripts be sold off by auction and his house be demolished.[23] Alfred de Musset had twenty people at his burial.[24] Barbey d'Aurevilly had to support himself in his old age by doing copy work right up until his last year.[25] Weiss passed away in near poverty.[26] Taine, our great, our admirable Taine, the loftiest literary figure of our age died over sixty years of age a simple chevalier de la Légion d'honneur![27] And it's not these masters France failed, but itself. She was able neither to exalt nor honour them any better when they were working. She could have prided herself upon them. I'd like to believe that with this new circumstance, what has to be done will be done, and that a public tribute will soon attest to what the countless readers of Maupassant know, which is that French literature has missed out in losing him whilst his pen was still capable of writing pages like those in this sketched out novel. But what a sketch and what a writer!

November 1894.

* The monument concerned now stands in the parc Monceau.[21] Is it permitted to regret that the Commitee hadn't chosen instead the jardin du Luxembourg, where today Maupassant would have neighboured some of the masters of the French novel: George Sand, Stendhal, and since this year, Flaubert (Note from 1922).[22]

The Angelus
[L'Angélus]

I [1]

The clock struck six and the Countess de Brémontal, her eyes wandering from the book she was reading, looked up at the dial of the handsome Louis XVI wall clock hung upon the wall; then she slowly swept her gaze over her large salon, sombre in spite of all the lamps—two on the table where lots of books languished, and two on the fireplace. A log fire, flaming in the hearth—a countryside fire, a château's fire—threw a broken glimmer upon the walls, lighting up the characters on the tapestries, the gold frames, the family portraits and casting the high curtains that draped and veiled the windows in a dark red light. In spite of all these lights the vast room was sad, slightly cold, invaded by the winter. From outside was felt the harsh rigour of the air and the breath of the wind frozen by the carpet of snow stretched out over the earth and making the trees in the park creak.

The countess rose; with the slightly slow, shuffling gait of a young pregnant woman, she came and sat down in front of the grate, holding her feet out to the flames. The blazing logs threw on them the emanation of their lively heat, a kind of burning, even slightly brutal, caress, whilst at the same time she felt her back, shoulders and neck continue to shiver with the frisson of the deathly atmosphere in which this terrible winter had enveloped France. This sensation of cold was slipping everywhere inside her, entering her soul as well as her body, and joined to this physical anguish was the immense catastrophe that had struck down the Country.

Tortured by her nerves, worries and agonizing presentiments, Mme de Brémontal got up again. Where is he at this hour, him, her husband, of whom she had received no news for five months? A prisoner of the Prussians or killed? Martyrized in an enemy fortress or interred in a hole on a battlefield with so many other corpses whose decomposing flesh mixed with the flesh of their neighbours and all the confused remains.

Oh! what horror! what horror!

Now she walked up and down the large silent salon, over the thick carpet that stifled the light noise of her steps. Never had she felt such terrifying anguish weigh upon her before. Was something else going to happen? Oh! the awful winter, the winter of the world's end that was destroying an entire country, killing the grown-up sons of poor mothers, the hope in their hearts and their last means of support, and killing the fathers of penniless children, and the husbands of young wives. She saw them dying, mutilated by guns, sabres, cannons, the iron-shod feet of horses that had passed over them, and shrouded on such nights as this by a winding sheet of snow stained with blood.

She felt as though she was going to cry, as though she was going to shout out, crushed by the fear of the unknowable tomorrow, and she looked at the time again. No, she wasn't just waiting for the moment when her father, the village priest and the doctor were to arrive, for they were dining at hers. But would they be able just to leave their houses and come over to the château? Her father was worrying her the most. He had to follow the tow path for several kilometres along the banks of the Seine in his coupé.[2] The coachman was old and trusty, knowing both the road and his horse; but this night seemed to be predestined to misfortunes. The two other invitees, regular visitors almost every evening moreover, had to cross the river by boat, which was even worse. The ice never stopped the current in this place where the sea's waves, which nothing can resist, rose with each tide; but enormous ice floes carried off in the eddy were descending from upper France and could capsize the ferryman's boat.

The countess came back to the fireplace, took the bell rope and rang.

An old servant appeared. She said to him:

'Is the little one asleep yet?'

'I don't think so, countess.'

'Tell Annette to bring him to me. I want to kiss him.'

'Yes, countess.'

The servant left. She called him back:

Chapter One

'Pierre!'

'Countess?'

'There isn't any danger in M. Boutemart coming by carriage along the water's edge for a while like tonight?'

The old Norman replied:

'None, countess. The coachman, Philippe, and his horse, Barbe, are both at ease with it and they know the path very well.'

Reassured about her father's fate, she asked again:

'And the gentlemen from La Bouille,[3] the priest and Dr Paturel, can they cross the water without peril in the midst of the floating ice floes?'

'Yes, yes, countess: old Pichard knows a thing or two and he won't be afraid of the ice packs. Plus he has a big boat in the winter on which occasionally he takes a cow or a horse.'

'Good', she said. 'Send down my little Henri.'

She sat back down at the table and opened a book.

It was *Les Contemplations* [*Contemplations*] and she fell, by chance, on these verses at the end of *La Fête chez Thérèse* ['Thérèse's Party']:

La nuit vint; tout se tut; les flambeaux s'éteignirent;
Dans les bois assombris les sources se plaignirent;
Le rossignol, caché dans son nid ténébreux,
Chanta comme un poète et comme un amoureux.
Chacun se dispersa sous les profonds feuillages,
Les folles en riant entraînèrent les sages;
L'amante s'en alla dans l'ombre avec l'amant;
Et, troublés comme on l'est en songe, vaguement,
Ils sentaient par degrés se mêler à leur âme,
A leurs discours secrets, à leurs regards de flamme,
A leur coeur, à leurs sens, à leur molle raison,
Le clair de lune bleu qui baignait l'horizon.

[Night came; all was silent; the torches died out;
Down in the gloomy woods the springs sighed out;
The nightingale, in its nest, in shadowy cover,

Sang out like a poet and sang out like a lover.
Everyone was spread out beneath the dense leaves,
The wise were led away by the laughing crazies;
Lover went off with lover into the shade;
And worried, like one is in a dream, so vague,
By degrees they felt themselves merge in their hearts,
With their secretive talks, and with a fiery glance,
In their hearts and their senses and their softened reason,
With the blue moonlight that bathed the entire horizon.]⁴

The countess's heart tightened with the thought that there were such nights as that and others like them. Why these contrasts, the charming sweetness and the ferocity of nature?

The door opened, she got up, and a young maid, a beautiful curvacious Norman girl, made to enter, holding by the hand a small four-year-old boy whose curly blond locks crowned him in a frizzy light beneath the glint from the lamps.

'Leave him with me until the gentlemen arrive', said the countess.

And when the chambermaid had left, she sat the child on her knees and looked him in the eyes. They smiled with that unique, inexpressible smile that signifies the love between a mother and her child, that love which alone is indestructible, which has no equal or rival.

Then, opening her arms, she took his head and kissed him. She kissed him on his hair, his eyelids, his mouth, trembling from the nape of her neck to the tips of her fingers with that delicious joy which resonates in those with the true maternal streak.

Then she cradled him, holding his neck. He asked in his delicate voice:

'Tell me, mummy, is daddy going to be back soon?'

She grabbed him, clasping him to her as though defending him, protecting him from the monstrous and distant danger of a war that could lay claim to him in turn.

And kissing him again, she whispered:

'Yes, my dear, soon. Oh! my love, what luck that you are so little! The wretches can't take you as well.'

What wretches was she speaking about? She couldn't have known to say.

Chapter One

But now the child who had a very keen ear distinguished in the distant night the faint noise of a small bell.

'Here's grandpapa!' he said.

'Where do you see grandpapa?' said the mother.

'That's the bell of his horsy.'

She heard it also and a little less worried at heart she stretched out her legs, as though alleviated, suddenly relaxed.

They were both now listening to the more distinct jingling and the blows of the coachman's whip resounding over the snow which announced their arrival.

A minute later the door opened to an old gentleman who maintained a fresh appearance in his handsome well-groomed person, with his clear cheeks and his white whiskers shining like silver.

He was tall, a little fat, with a well-to-do appearance. He was still known as handsome Boutemart. He was the typical merchant, the industrial Norman who had made a big fortune. Nothing dented his excellent humour, his unshakeable cool, his absolute confidence in himself. Since the war only one thing preoccupied him deeply, and that was no longer seeing smoke go into the sky from the four chimneys of his two big factories from which he had grown rich from chemical products. At first he had believed in victory with the jingoist's boasting and the robust confidence with which all of bourgeois France was inflated before the fatal year of 1870. Now, during the bloody defeats, the debacles, the retreats, he murmured with the unwavering conviction of a man who has always succeeded in his projects: 'Bah! It's a great hardship, but France always gets back on its feet again.'

His daughter ran to him with open arms, whilst little Henri grabbed one of his hands. Lots of kisses were exchanged.

She asked:

'Anything new?'

'Yes. They say the Prussians have entered Rouen today. General Briant's army is falling back on Le Havre by the left bank.[5] They must now be at Pont-Audemer.[6] A fleet of barges and steam boats are waiting for them at Honfleur[7] to transport them to Le Havre.'

The countess shivered. What! the Prussians were so near, they were in the neighbourhood, at Rouen, just a few leagues away!

She murmured:

The Angelus

'Then we're in great danger, father.'

He replied:

'Certainly we're not in absolute safety. But they have orders to always respect harmless inhabitants and the houses which haven't been abandoned. If it wasn't for this rule which they always observe, I would've come and settled in here. But an old man like me wouldn't be of much service to you and I can save my factories. Whether they do or don't find me near you, as we mustn't resist or cause trouble, there are more risks leaving Dieppedalle to come here.'[8]

Frightened and full of trepidation, she murmured:

'But all alone in this château, I'd lose my head in the midst of those brutes.'

Understanding in truth that it was impossible to leave his daughter alone in the face of this terrible and immanent threat—something which he still hadn't envisaged, the idea striking him with force for the first time, he replied:

'All the same, you are right. There isn't any danger this evening, for they're not going to venture into the night on their arrival in this unknown region. I will return to Dieppedalle to make arrangements and tomorrow I'll come and put up here, and I'll stay here until the end of the occupation.'

She hugged him, knowing with her keen woman's observation, which understood him clearly, what an immense sacrifice he was making for her in abandoning his factories, and she said:

'Thank you, dad.'

The little maid Annette entered, looking for the child; and the gaze of M. Boutemart upon her, which was most discreet, almost imperceptible, and which the sly Norman girl returned, made the countess blush a little red on her pale cheeks, for she was beginning to suspect her father's attention towards the servant and the consent of the latter.

Since the death of his wife, after just nine years, M. Boutemart, who never left Dieppedale and his chemical establishments, had had a few relationships in the area, discovered by chance, and revealing his unfussy, almost vulgar, tastes, and from which Mme de Brémontal suffered greatly, in her daughter's pride and in that petty vanity of the nobility that had very lightly entered into her when she became the region's countess and lady of the manor.

Little Henri kissed his mother and grandfather, then he left blowing still more kisses.

Chapter One

As he was leaving the front doorbell rang, announcing the arrival of the last two guests. They made their appearance. Abbé Marvaux entered first, tall, thin, upright, with a face marked with deep wrinkles on the forehead and the cheeks. When you saw him you guessed that this man suffered a lot and that he must have been eaten away by the soul of a melancholy thinker, one of those souls that has early on turned the face into a weary mask.

Of noble origin, for he was named M. de Marvaux, he was related in a very distant way to the Brémontals. He had started life in a military career, as much to occupy his idleness as in response to the need for violent action, combat, and the vague heroism that he felt within him. Instructed and nurtured on philosophy, he soon experienced a great ennui towards the idle garrison life, and it was with pleasure that he left in 1859 for the Italian campaign.[9] He took part, bravely, in several battles, but in a bizarre change of mind, by one of those strange anomalies that sometimes place in beings the most opposed and contradictory instincts, the sight of the massacres, of troops of men pulverized by volleys of grapeshot, soon gave him a horror and hatred of war. He was however noticed and decorated there, and he obtained the rank of captain; but once the campaign was over, he tendered his resignation.

After a few years of a free life occupied with studies and lectures, a few published pamphlets, for he loved things of the mind, he met a young widow who pleased him and married her. He had a daughter with her; then the mother and the child died, in the same week, of typhoid fever.

What happened inside him? What strange mysticism awoke in his spirit after this dismal event? He took orders and became a priest; and from the day when he dressed in the black cassock, he never wore the red ribbon won on the field of battle, calling it his bloodstain.

He could have had in this new career a great sacerdotal future; he preferred to remain a country priest in his home region. Perhaps also the independence of his character, his brazen speech, made him suspect to the diocese. For he had stood up to the bishop several times in theological and dogmatic discussions, and as he was extremely erudite and eloquent, he triumphed in these battles.

Without ambition, and moreover, having lost his zest for everything, he made up his mind or resigned himself to living in this beautiful land which he adored, and, as he possessed a certain fortune, he did very well there. He was liked and respected. He became a generous priest, helpful to everyone, unique in the region, where popular veneration protected and defended him from the growing ill will and suspicions of his superiors.

Doctor Paturel, who followed him, was a little potbellied man who would have been completely bald if he hadn't kept on his temples, on the edge of the skull, two patches of frizzy white hair, like two powder puffs of rice.

As soon as they entered, it was announced that dinner was served, and the Countess de Brémontal, taking the doctor's arm, went into the dining room.

Barely had they sat down in front of their soup when the priest asked:

'Do you know that they're at Rouen?'

They mumbled 'Yes' in reply to him. Then M. Boutemart questioned:

'Have you recent details?'

'A few. Three corps of the invading army appeared, at exactly the same time, at three of the city gates, and the vanguards convened at the place de l'Hôtel-de-Ville, almost at the same instant.' [10]

The doctor added:

'Yesterday I was at Bourg-Achard [11] when I saw the French army pass in retreat.'

And they discussed a mass of details, in hushed tones, as if they were feeling around them something of the presence of the formidable conquerors.

'Today,' said the priest, 'this is the first time since I left the army that I regret no longer being a soldier.'

The young woman, shaken with anguish, asked:

'Do you think they will come through here?'

Abbé Marvaux asserted it, then resumed:

'Are you still without news of your husband, countess?'

She mumbled in despair:

'Yes, monsieur le curé.'

But Boutemart, always convinced that the events which were touching them would end up turning out alright, added:

'Bah! he's a prisoner. He will return after the war.'

The countess stammered:

'Prisoner... or dead.'

Her father, irritated by sad ideas, had a fit of impatience.

Chapter One

'Why do you make up such inventions? You live in the expectation of misfortune as if there was nothing else upon the earth.'

Abbé Marvaux whispered:

'There's hardly anything else, however, monsieur, when we look close around us. Think of France at the moment.'

Boutemart didn't agree.

'But no, no: take me, I have never been unfortunate.'

His daughter said to him sadly:

'It's only because you have desired and sought out fortune that you have had it.'[12]

He started to laugh:

'Of course! One has everything with fortune. The rest is a joke. But in the present case, it is undoubted that the lists of the dead have been established almost everywhere and already communicated to their families. As for prisoners, we can't know who they are.'

She groaned:

'There are also the missing persons.'

And Boutemart with aptness replied:

'They are the revenants of tomorrow.'

The doctor joined in the conversation:

'Me, I'm fairly lucky,' he said, 'I know where my son is. He is in Faidherbe's army,[13] and we exchange letters. What's more, I was lucky that he qualified as a doctor before the war, as the doctors don't have a great deal to fear in the army. But all that I say doesn't prevent my wife from being in an awful state, for she loves him so much, her dear Jules.'

He praised his son, whose medical studies in Paris had been so brilliant that all of his professors, after he had passed his doctorate, together encouraged him to continue to his agrégation.[14] Ah! there's one who won't stagnate in the country, that young one there. He could become a great doctor, a great doctor of the capital.

And the conversation drawled on, no matter what subject, paralyzed by this idea of the invasion which hung over them.

After the men had had their coffees and smoked their cigars, they returned to the salon, close to the countess, who was toasting her feet by the fire. She was nevertheless cold, cold throughout, in the heart and in the body.

The Angelus

M. Boutemart was the first to speak about going. His factories were preoccupying him and he asked for his carriage at half past nine under the pretext that at a time like this he shouldn't be returning at too late an hour. The other two followed his lead, putting on some boots in order to cross the snow and reach the ferry on the banks of the Seine, and the countess remained alone.

She leafed through a few books without taking any great interest in them, barely understanding what she was reading. She chose those poets and pieces of verse which she returned to most often. They seemed banal, pointless and colourless to her; and she sat back down in front of the fire. Was she going to go to bed? no, not straight away, for she wouldn't be able to sleep; she experienced those interminable periods of insomnia, which were painful and became a nocturnal agony for mind and body, measuring out the regular ringing of the clock's bell.

And so she reflected. Memories of herself and of old came back to her, intimate memories evoked by the gloomy hours, secrets about herself that she told no one else.

She remembered her childhood in this same region, in her parents' house at Dieppedalle, built in front of the factory, her mother, her good mother, her dear mother, whom she had seen die. And she cried, her hands over her eyes.

Her father, a small merchant at first, the heir to a large piece of land on the banks of the Seine, and a manufactory of acids and artificial vinegars, had ended up earning a great fortune from chemical products. He had married the daughter of an officer of the First Empire, a young pretty little thing, independent and poetic, as they were in that era. Also a little melancholy after this union which didn't fulfil her youthful dreams, she consoled herself with a love of what is still called 'Nature', using the sense of the word that is almost forgotten today.[15] She loved this superb land, planted with trees and sprayed with water, this coastline, at the foot of which smoked the chimneys of her husband, but which also bore on its summit the admirable forest of Roumare stretching from Rouen to Jumièges.[16] What's more she began to compile a library of novels, philosophers, and poets, and she spent her life in reading and dreaming. In the evening, at dusk, walking along the Seine full of green islands plumed with great poplars, she recited in hushed tones, for herself, and herself alone, the verse of Chénier and Lamartine. Soon she developed enthusiasm for Victor Hugo, she adored Musset.[17] Having become the mother of a daughter, she brought her up with an ardent tenderness, a

Chapter One

tenderness augmented sentimentally by all the literature upon which she had been nurtured.

The child grew up, greatly resembling her mother, charming and intelligent. They were envied in Rouen and it was said of Mme Boutemart: 'She's a person of great worth.'

The little girl, whom she educated with an impassioned care, aided by a governess, was by sixteen already a young person with the air of a little lady, a brunette with violet eyes, the exact colour of the flowers of the periwinkle, such a rare hue.

And the child almost an adult, whose mother had let her read a great deal already, developed her young soul and her nascent sensibility in the same way. Sometimes she opened other books secretly, those that she wasn't allowed, and she already knew by heart certain verses which seemed to her as sweet as perfumes, musical sounds or the breaths of the wind.

These people were entirely happy, or almost entirely, when, during a very cold winter, after an overlong walk in the snow-filled forest, Mme Boutemart had to take to bed, suffering from pneumonia which carried her off within a week.

Remaining alone with his daughter, the father wondered if he shouldn't keep her close to him, for he would be completely alone, completely abandoned in this countryside, in the middle of his workers and machines.

But his sister, a childless widow of an engineer from the Department of Civil Engineering,[18] possessed of sufficient wealth, agreed to leave Paris for a few months to come and spend them near him and assuage the first attacks of sorrow and isolation.

She was a woman as level-headed as her brother and of composed sense, who had always turned events and things to as good account as possible. At ease with her fate, having passed forty, and endowed with a calm nature, she asked for nothing more of destiny.

She quickly fell in love with her niece and when Boutemart spoke to her of keeping the young girl close to him she dissuaded him of it with all her force by representing to him that Germaine would become very much sought after when marriageable. Above all he must complete her education and upbringing as perfectly as possible. That could only be done in Paris. She would be a very good match and she had to be ignorant of nothing that she should know, such as serious-minded acquaintances to begin with, and then the arts of charm, dance, music, and more such things which complete the dowry of a rich girl. And so he placed her in a large boarding school, and the aunt took care of seeing her often, very often, to take her out every week, and even to keep her with her for a few days from time to time.

This woman, whose husband had been in high offices under the Minister of Public Works, [19] maintained good connections in her widowhood, and she was very well thought of. Her brother, understanding all the advantages of this combination, accepted it thus, and at the beginning of spring the aunt took the niece off with her.

She entered her into one of those elegant fashionable boarding schools where well-born orphans are raised and where wealthy foreigners are kept whilst their parents are travelling. She had a pretty apartment there, a chambermaid, and top quality teachers. She also had classes in town, those classes for young ladies where half the young girls of Paris, those from the bourgeoisie and nobility, the demi-rich, rich and very rich, meet and make acquaintances for later.

Her aunt came and found her to take her for walks, amuse her, show her the town, the monuments, the museums. The cruel melancholy with which Germaine had remained saturated since the death of her mother seemed, at last, to be slightly assuaged. Her pretty violet eyes, beneath eyelids that had often turned red from tears of remembering her greatly loved mother, were recovering their fresh violet tones.

However she thought a lot about the house at Dieppedalle, where her father stayed alone, and she missed the space, the countryside and the freedom.

She was already familiar with that small everlasting nostalgia of the uprooted, who suffer from it when they are imprisoned in the cities by their duties or their professions, almost all of whose lungs, eyes and skin have had for their first nourishment the great sky and the pure air of the fields and whose little feet first ran on tracks through the woods, paths in the meadows and grassy banks.

Even the children of Paris exiled to provincial professions or offices suffer, all their life, as though from a physical privation, of an irresistible need for pavements and big roads streaming with people.

When the holidays came, Germaine left with glee for Normandy; and it was heartache when, in the autumn, she returned to Paris. She spent three winters there, from sixteen to nineteen years of age. Then M. Boutemart took her back to soften his widower's isolation.

Chapter One

    Then a marriage plan came to him for his daughter. He knew her taste was in favour of the countryside where she had grown up, and for him it would be of great benefit if he could discover the means of fixing and keeping her in his neighbourhood, a benefit of wellbeing, affection, sentiment, indulgence, and of a selfishness satisfied to the end of his life.

    And usually he was skilful enough to unearth around him what he needed.

    Through his relations with the conseil général,[20] of which they were both members, and through the neighbourhood and hunting, he had known for a long time one of his neighbours, the Count de Brémontal, owner of the château du Bec, at Sahurs, opposite La Bouille, only a few kilometres from Dieppedalle.[21] He was a man of twenty-eight years, orphaned of father and mother, master of a handsome landed fortune, good looking, an excellent rider and a great huntsman. All his ambition and pleasure in life consisted in good administration of his vast properties, rearing cattle and cultivation. He was very good at it, driven by that love of the soil so strong in the hearts of Normans. He had the spirit of the region about him—a little ponderous, but merry, and the proper, even distinguished, air of a country gentleman capable of putting on a good show everywhere.

    Boutemart cherished him, made a fuss of him, won him over, became his friend, his hunting and leisure companion. They dined at each other's houses often, and when the young girl returned home altogether to her father's house, she found this agreeable neighbour installed there almost as if in his own home.

    He made a very good impression on her. She seemed charming to him. They took horse rides together and made long excursions into the forest of Roumare, always followed by a groom for the sake of respectability.

    Walks were organized, outings in the country, village fêtes with all the appropriate families of the region. He finally fell in love with her, began to court her and soon awoke the desires to please, seduce, and conquer which sleep in the hearts of young girls. She was pleasant, then coquettish, and the simple man that he was loved her very ardently. After six months of attentions he made his proposal. Germaine was consulted and agreed, and the father said 'yes' with all his heart.

    They were a good couple to whom only one son came after five years of marriage.

    The countess loved her child with an extreme maternal affection. It revealed a powerful unsuspected instinct within her, just there in her flesh, and she wanted others.

The Angelus

Above all she wanted a daughter, to raise her in accordance with her soul, her tastes, her ideal of woman.

Her desire wasn't quickly realized, she grew sad, worried, and, troubled before this ungraspable dream, addressed heaven with her wife's complaint. A type of strange and mystical devotion pushed her towards Mary, patron of mothers. She didn't implore her, as fanatics implore, with words and formulas, but she sent her from the depth of her heart a tender and constant prayer.

She wasn't a devotee, wasn't even an ardent believer, having been brought up by a father indifferent to these things and a mother almost incredulous. Mme Boutemart, in effect, born in the era where the great moral, philosophical and religious battles of the Revolution had made pious beliefs disappear in a lot of families, throughout her life held independent opinions that her father had inculcated her with.

Her daughter Germaine was however baptized and made her first communion, but she received from her mother no further doctrine or religious fervour.

Now, after she had lost her mother and spent three years in the elegant Paris boarding school where she completed her education across the board, she learnt Christian faith just as she did history or music. The main priest tasked with leading the souls of these young ladies towards God was a smart man, ingratiating, persuasive and domineering. When he discovered the undecided and nonchalant views of Germaine, he dedicated himself to converting her with the tenacity of a missionary. He only succeeded in making her a demi-devotee, but one who soon believed with all her heart and all her imagination in the touching Christian legend.

She had bouts of sentimental tenderness and gentle surges of piety towards the Saviour and his mother, the Virgin, but she was never overcome with the practices of worship which she deemed as being meant for the uneducated classes. She lent herself to it however from good will, attending mass on Sundays, and fulfilling her obligatory duties as much through conscience as appearance.

So she asked of the Virgin Mary, mother of Christ, a child, a daughter; her wishes weren't granted, and the war of 1870, brusquely declared, had more influence in satisfying this wish than her implorations to heaven.

Although exempt from the obligations of military service, M. de Brémontal, an ardent patriot, at the first news of France being in danger, wanted to head off and enlist. Germaine, who loved him greatly, without great passion, but as a faithful

Chapter One

and devoted companion, more like a mother than a wife, had an awful fear of losing him, for she wanted nothing other than to end life by his side, in this château which she liked, in this region which she adored, with her children about her.

The thought of the dangers that he was going to run, the possibility of his death, the worry from which she would suffer during this perilous absence, made her decide to try everything, to do everything, think of anything to wear out his resolution.

What did she do? What all pretty young women have tried; she became tender once more with subtle coquetries so lithe that he was overcome as if by a new love. She found once more, for her husband whose heart was being carried away to a great duty, unexpected wifely enticements, which she fastened and gave up like a smitten mistress.

She had never been like that for him before, never had he felt from her this troubling attraction, the so captivating charm of kisses which made forgotten and consented to everything. And he suddenly discovered this passionate abandon in his wife with a delighted astonishment. Conquered, at first he gave himself up to all the affections, to all the caresses, to all the dexterity of love with which she entwined and enchained him.

But when the rout of the French armies became irretrievable, when the great disasters were made known, when the ruin of the country was imminent, the heart of the patriotic gentleman beat stronger than the heart of the lover. The son of the old Norman seigneurs,[22] the heir of their bravery and their adventurous audacity, he felt, he understood, that he had to provide an example of courage for those around him, and he left brusquely one morning, with tears in eyes and despair in the heart.

For several weeks she received letters from her husband, and she learnt that he had been able to join up with the army of General Chanzy who was still fighting.[23] Then all the news stopped. Then she fell ill, and here it was that one day, which at any other time would have been such a great happiness, the doctor revealed to her after a consultation that she was going to be a mother.

Oh! what terrible months she spent, five months of appalling anguishes during which she heard nothing from him!

Was he dead or a prisoner?

This phrase, always the same, haunted her thought, obsessed her nights and days.

And even now she repeated it whilst walking from one end of the salon to the other.

The hours and half hours rang out one after the other on the bell of the wall clock, and the countess resolved not to go up. A distress more poignant than those of other nights, a type of sinister presentiment oppressed her soul. She sat down, got up, started to dream, then, weary in spirit as well as body, she carried the cushions from the divan and made with her big armchair a sort of bed in front of the fire in order to try and sleep there for a little while, as her bedroom made her scared.

Her eyes were finally growing heavy and her thoughts were growing numb amidst this tumult of life which passes away, this existence annihilated by sleep, when a strange unknown noise made her shudder and straighten up.

She listened, breathless. There were voices getting nearer, the voices of men. And so, running to the window, she half-opened it to better hear behind the canopy. She heard the steps of horses in the snow, a sound of metal, of sabres clanging; and the voices, getting closer and closer, speaking foreign words.

Them! It was the Prussians!

She rushed to the hand bell and rang it, rang it with all her strength, as one sounds the tocsin for pressing dangers. Then the image of her child, of her little Henri, struck like a bullet to her heart, she rushed up the staircase towards his room.

The servants, awoken, were rushing up, candles in hand, barely dressed: the footman, the coachman, a servant girl, a cook and the nanny.

The countess cried:

'The Prussians! the Prussians!'

At the same moment a knock shook the main door so strong that it was like the impact of a battering ram; and a powerful voice shouted from outside a command in German, that no one inside understood.

And so Mme de Brémontal ordered two old servants:

'To avoid violence, we mustn't resist them. Go quickly and open up to them, and give them what they want. Me, I'm going to shut myself up with my son. If they ask about me, say I'm ill, incapable of coming down.'

Another blow shook the door, and made the whole château vibrate. Still another followed it, then another, and another. They resounded in the corridor like cannons. Voices shouted outside the walls; it was like a siege had begun.

Chapter One

The countess and Annette disappeared into the little boy's bedroom, whilst the two men went down with haste to open up to the invaders, and the cook and the serving girl, overcome with fear, remained standing on the steps of the staircase in order to await the events, and to flee through any open exit.

When Mme de Brémontal opened the curtains of Henri's bed, he was sleeping, having heard nothing in his trouble-free sleep. His mother, waking him up, didn't know what to say to him without upsetting him too much or terrifying him by announcing the presence of the villainous men who were downstairs and armed.

When, beneath her kisses, he had opened his eyes, she told him that the soldiers that were passing through the country had entered the château; and as he had often heard talk of the war, he asked:

'Are they the enemy soldiers, mummy?'

'Yes, my child, the enemy soldiers.'

'Do you know if they've seen daddy?'

She received a terrible shock to the heart and answered:

'I don't know darling.'

She and Annette dressed him, quickly, covering him with the warmest clothes, for nothing could be known, nothing foreseen.

The battering ram blows had stopped. Now only a loud stirring of voices and clinking of sabres in the interior of the château were heard. It was the taking of possession, the invasion of the dwelling, the violation of the sacred intimacy of the home.

The countess trembled on hearing it, and felt awaken within her a furious revolt of anger and indignation. Her home. They were in her home, these hated Prussians, absolute masters, free to do anything, with the power even to kill.

There were sudden raps knocking at her door.

She asked:

'Who is there?'

The voice of her footman replied:

'It's me, countess.'

She opened. The servant appeared, and she whispered:

'Well?'

'Well, they want Madame to come down.'

'I don't want to.'

The Angelus

'They said if Madame wouldn't, they'd come up and look for her.'

She wasn't scared. All of her sang-froid had returned to her with the courage of an exasperated woman. It was war, oh well! she would behave like a man.

'Tell them that I won't take orders from them and that I'll stay here.'

Pierre hesitated, having understood that the commanding officer was a brute.

But she repeated in a very firm tone: 'Go', which he obeyed. She didn't turn the key behind him in order not to have the appearance of hiding, and she waited, shaking.

Some heavy steps soon mounted the staircase, those of several men, and again, there was a knock on the door.

She asked:

'Who is there?'

A foreign voice pronounced:

'A Prussian officer.'

'Enter,' she said.

A young, well-built man presented himself, saluted, and, in good French, almost without accent [said]:

'Would you please excuse me, madame, if I carry out the order of my superior, who has given me the task of bringing you to him. Do you want to come down willingly? It would be better for you to do so, for you, and for us.'

She hesitated a second, then:

'Yes, monsieur, I will follow you.'

And calling her servant standing behind the officer:

'Take the little one in your arms and follow me. I don't want us to be separated.'

The man obeyed and followed her, carrying her son. And so she passed in front of the Prussian and descended slowly, hampered by her size, supporting herself with the banister, and Annette remained alone in the bedroom, too paralyzed with terror to make the least movement.

On arriving at the entrance to the salon she noticed seven or eight officers, already settled in as though at home, the troops being in the village. They were smoking, lounging in the armchairs, sabres thrown on the table, on the books, on the poets, whilst two orderlies guarded the door.

She noticed the sergeant at first glance, back to the fire, a sole raised to the flame. He had kept on his uniform's cap, and his face hairy with a red beard seemed to glow with joy in the victory and pleasure of being warm.

Chapter One

On seeing her enter he made a slight military salute, impertinent and brief, without taking off his hat, then he said with a German pronunciation that seemed thick with sauerkraut and sausage:

'You are za lady of zis château?'[24]

She stood in front of him, without having returned his insolent salute, and she responded with a 'yes' so curt that all eyes turned from the woman to the soldier.

He was unmoved and replied:

'How many persons are zer here?'

'I have two old servants, three maids, and three farmhands.'

'Your husband, vot does he do? Ver is he?'

She boldly replied:

'He is a soldier, like you, and he is fighting.'

The officer retorted with insolence:

'Vell! he is now beaten.'

And he laughed a big beardy laugh. When he laughed, two or three others laughed, as heartily, in those different timbres which set the tone of Teutonic mirth. The others fell silent on examining attentively this courageous Frenchwoman.

And so she said, braving the sergeant with an intrepid look:

'Monsieur, you are not a gentleman, coming and insulting a woman in her own home, as you do.'

A long silence followed, very long, terrible. The German soldier remained impassive, always laughing, authoritatively able to have everything to his taste.

'But no,' he said, 'you aren't in your home; you are in our home. Zer is no longer anyvon at home in France.'

And he laughed again, with the delighted certainty of confirming there and then an incontestable and staggering truth.

Exasperated, she responded:

'Violence isn't a right. It's a heinous crime. You are no more at home than a thief in a burgled house.'

An anger lit up the eyes of the Prussian.

'I vill prove zat you are not at home. For I order you to leave zis house, or indeed I vill chase you from it.'

The Angelus

At the sound of this spiteful voice, harsh and strong, little Henri, more amazed up until then by these men than frightened, began to let forth some piercing cries.

Hearing the child cry, the countess lost her head and the idea of the brutalities which this army rabble might let leash, dangers that her dear little one could face, sent a mad wish straight to her heart, to set off, to flee no matter where, to a little cottage in the village. Thrown outdoors. So much the better! ....

[II] [1]

[List of possible character names]

Morvaux, Cormusel, De la Charlerie, Charlery, Doctor Parizot, Abbé de Praxeville, Antoine de Praxas, Brémontal, Courmarin, Hiral, Marmelin, Boutemare, la famille et les demoiselles de Cerisaie [the de Cerisaie family and daughters], Abbé Marvaux, Doctor Paturel, ferryman Pichard, coachman Philippe...

[Portrait of Doctor Paturel Jr]

His face slightly resembled the lean visage of Voltaire and Bonaparte. [2] He had a sharp, bent, angular, pointed nose, a strong jaw with jutting bones beneath the ears, and a tapered chin; pale grey eyes with the black stains of the pupils in the middle, and such an air of authority in his speech and his professional demonstrations that he inspired great confidence in everyone. He brought about the recoveries of people for a long time known as incurable, rheumatics, rural ankylotics, the infirm from humidity, by methods of hygiene, nutrition and exercise, and powders which restore appetites; he healed old wounds with new antiseptics and persecuted the microbe according to the most recent procedures. [3] Then when he had treated a patient, he seemed to leave cleanliness behind him in the house. He prospered, they called for him from great distances, and the money came, for that's where he got it, setting the price of his visits according to distance and wealth.

[III] [1]

[Discussion between Doctor Paturel Jr and Abbé Marvaux in the presence of André, the second crippled son of Mme de Brémontal]

'You are the premier doctor in the département... wealth, the lot.'
'But living here', he said, 'I'm sapped, I'm losing my life; everything that I love and that I wish for I don't have. Ah! Paris, Paris!... Can I work for me here, work for science? Do I have laboratories, hospitals, rare cases, all the known and unknown diseases of the entire world under my eyes? Can I carry out experiments, reports, become a member of the Académie de médecine?[2] Here I have nothing, neither future, nor diversions, neither pleasure, nor a woman to marry or to love, nor glory to gather, nothing, nothing but the glory of the arrondissement. I cure, yes, I cure people, miserly bourgeois who pay in silver, sometimes in gold, and never in notes. I cure the little miser of the common people, but never princes, ambassadors, ministers, great artists, the resounding cure of whom is repeated in the heart of foreign courts. In the provincial depths I treat and I cure, in a word, the dregs of society.'

The priest listened to him with a bit of a tense and angry air.
He muttered:
'That is perhaps nobler, grander, more beautiful.'
But the doctor, livid, resumed:
'I don't live for others, I live for me, monsieur le curé.'
The abbé felt his apostle's heart tremble. He added:
'Christ died for the little people.'
And the doctor snorted:

The Angelus

'But I am not Christ, Gordon Bennett! [3] I am Doctor Paturel, agrégé of the Faculté de médecine of Paris.' [4]

The abbé, calmed, replied having spent a few seconds in a cycle of ideas almost reaching the limits of human thought, for he saw all the magnanimity and meanness of the absolute. And he concluded:

'Perhaps you are right. From your point of view you are in the right. And for you, that's the only good.'

'Of course!' the doctor hurled out in a clear voice, which rang out in the dry air.

Then the priest added:

'You do however have a big heart, for here you stay for your mother.'

The doctor trembled; his soft spot had been touched, his weakness, his private tenderness.

'Yes, I will never leave her.'

Together their eyes fell on the cripple who was all ears listening to them and understood them very well.

And the glances of these two men having met said mysterious things about the destiny and future of the child, when compared to theirs. The pitiful wretch was him.

But thought of Christ haunted the abbé. He resumed the conversation:

'Personally, I love Christ.'

The doctor riposted:

'Monsieur le curé, ever since this world existed, all the gods conceived by human thought have been monsters. Was it not Voltaire who said: "Scripture claims that God made man in his own image, we have certainly returned the compliment"?' [5]

He accumulated the proofs, the injustices, the ferocities, the wrongdoings of Providence. He added:

'For me who is a doctor of these poor people, I see them, these wrongdoings, I observe them everyday. You too, moreover, who cares for their souls. If I had to write a book, a collection of documents on that subject, I would call it: 'The Dossier of God': and it would be terrible, monsieur le curé.'

The Abbé Marvaux sighed:

'We can do nothing to penetrate these questions and mysteries beyond our cerebral faculties. Personally, I don't believe that I can understand God. He is too

Fragment Three

expansive and universal for our minds. The word God represents some conception and explanation, a refuge from doubts, a sanctuary from fear, a consolation from death, a remedy from selfishness. It's a formula of religious phraseology, God: not a God… Us men, we can only love a tangible and visible God. The other, the unknown, the unknowable, the immense something, we haven't been given a sense to comprehend it, through pity for our hearts we were sent Christ.'

The priest, wild-eyed, fell silent; then, following his unique thought, he mumbled:

'Who knows? Perhaps Christ was also misled in his mission by God, as we are. But he became God himself for the world, for our miserable world, for our little world covered with the long-suffering and the churls. He is God, our God, my God, and I love him with all my human heart and my priest's soul. O lord crucified on the Calvary, I am yours, your son and servant!'

The doctor, surprised, muttered:

'It's so strange what you just said!'

'Yes', resumed the priest, 'Christ must also be God's victim. He received a false mission, that of deluding us through a new religion. But the divine Messenger accomplished it so easily, this mission, so magnificent, so devoted, so painful, so unimaginably great and touching, that for us he took the place of his Inspirer. What is God, vague word, before Christ? Us who know nothing and are bound to nothing except through our poor organs, can we worship these letters in which we cannot understand the meaning, this shadowy God of which we conceive nothing, neither existence, nor intention, nor power, of which we only know a small clumsy, contemptible attempt at creation, the world, a kind of penal colony for souls tormented with knowledge, and for bodies in bad health? No, we cannot love that. But Christ, in whom is all pity, all magnanimity, all philosophy, all knowledge of humanity descended from we don't know where, who was more unfortunate than the most wretched, who was born in a stable and died nailed to a tree trunk, leaving us the only word of truth which is wise and consoling for living in this sad place, that, that is my God, for me, that's my God.'

A sigh beside him made him shut up. André was crying in his wheelchair.

The priest kissed him on his forehead. The young man stammered:

'How I love to hear you speak! I understand you perfectly.'

And the priest answered him:

The Angelus

'Poor little one, you also, you have received from merciless destiny a sad lot. But you will at least have, I believe, in compensation for all the physical joys, the only beautiful things which have been allowed to men—dream, intelligence and thought.'..

[IV] [1]

[*Meditation on God*]

Eternal murderer who seems only to taste the pleasure of creating in order to savour tirelessly his relentless passion of killing anew, of beginning again his exterminations as he creates beings. Eternal producer of corpses and supplier of cemeteries, who, after sowing the grains and scattering the germs of life in order to ceaselessly satisfy his insatiable need for destruction, has a good laugh. Murderer hungry for death taking cover in Space to create and destroy beings, mutilate them, impose all sufferings upon them, strike them with all illnesses, like a tireless destructor who continues ceaselessly his horrible work. He invented cholera, the plague, typhus, all of the microbes which eat away at the body. Only the beasts, however, are ignorant of the ferocity, for they are unaware of this law of death which menaces them as us. The horse which gambols under the sun in a prairie, the goat which climbs rocks with her light and subtle gait, followed by the billy goat that pursues her, the pigeons which bill and coo on the roofs, the doves beak in beak beneath the verdure of the trees, like lovers expressing their affections, and the nightingale singing in the moonlight, near his mate who broods not knowing the eternal massacre of this God who created them. The sheep who..

Auguste Dorchain's account of *The Angelus* [1]

In August 1892,[2] I was at Champel-les-Bains,[3] near Geneva, seeking a cure for nervous exhaustion from the iced waters of l'Arve[4] and the invigorating air of the heights, when one day I was informed of the visit of Guy de Maupassant, whom Doctor Cazalis—the poet Jean Lahor[5]—had brought to the thermal establishment.

'I brought him here,' he told me aside from our mutual friend, 'to make him believe that, like you, he only had a bit of neurasthenia and so that you might tell him that this treatment has already greatly relieved and fortified you. Alas! his illness is not the same as yours, that won't take you long in seeing.'

Maupassant had under his arm a barrister's briefcase, full of papers. He opened it and showed me the pages.

'Here are the first fifty pages of my novel: *The Angelus*. For the last year I haven't been able to write on anything else. If, in three months, the book isn't finished, I'll kill myself.'

Those were his first words. Am I going to speak of all that he said in addition, all of it in an incessant stream of language and with a fixed stare equally as frightening, that he told me during the three days that he could be kept at Champel? Certainly not! the memory of it is too cruel for me and it's not something that should be left to anyone. I prefer to remember only one admirable evening, when, for two hours, I could believe him cured, saved, when he became his level self once more. We had, my wife and I, invited him to dinner in our little chalet, annexed to the Hôtel des Bains:[6] he brought his manuscript from which he was

The Angelus

hardly ever separated, having decided that in there was his sentence, and he said to us:

'I'm going to tell you *The Angelus*.'

He told it with extraordinary lucidity, logic, eloquence and emotion. It was, if my memory is faithful, the story of a woman on the verge of becoming a mother, and whose husband, a soldier, has left her alone in the family château, during the Année Terrible [Terrible Year].[7] A winter's night, Christmas eve, the Prussians invade the house; after resistance or a complaint, they consign the poor woman to the stable after having maltreated and even injured her; and on the straw, whilst the church bells ring in the distance, she brings forth into the world a son, as in bygone days did the Virgin Mary. But what a son! an injured son, crippled forever by the blow that his mother received, a son with shattered legs who would never walk and who would never be a man like other men. The years pass for him without any cure, but they refine his soul through the infinitely tender love of his mother, as if to make him capable of suffering still more. Did Jesus really come into the world to bring joy?... One day, when he has become a young man, a young girl passes by and the cripple adores her, with his great and tender heart, but without being able to tell her, and without her being able to love him. It's his older brother, his handsome able-bodied brother, that she loves, and the two of them present the torturing spectacle of their happiness to the poor wretch.

'Come now, my darling,' said the mother, cradling him like a little child, 'I will take you away to a beautiful land, I will read you beautiful books, you will forget, you'll be happy too, that's what I want, that's what I want...'

And the poor child shook his head.[8] And that was what happened; and everywhere, and always, he must see pass in front of his eyes, until the day when he closed them to the light, this charming phantom which he would never get close to, ever: a young girl.

And Maupassant cried on finishing his piece, which lasted two hours, and we also cried, seeing what still remained of the genius, tenderness and pity of this soul, which never more would fully express itself, taking hold of other souls...

The narrative broached the greatest depths of human distress; but one felt that if one day he was able to write it, the thinker would be immediately, powerfully and desperately crushed, like a diver who drowns, by the sinister substance of his thought, and that he would come back up again in one movement towards the light and towards hope... That was a certainty if he was cured; for on that occasion, in his accent, and in his words, and with his tears, Maupassant had something of the religious that bypassed the horror of life and the sombre terror of non-existence...

But he wasn't cured; the *Angelus* didn't progress a page further; and a few months later we learnt that at Nice, on board his yacht *Bel-Ami*, the great writer had tried to cut open his own throat... .[9]

Hermine Lecomte du Noüy's account of *The Angelus* [1]

[Hermine Lecomte du Noüy:] '[...] Have you read the fragment of the 'Angelus' which was published in the *Revue de Paris*?'

[Henri Amic:] 'Yes, but I've forgotten it. I remember that this unfinished work left me with a great sadness.'

'Maupassant had told me the plan of this novel in a very detailed manner; he even read to me chapters which haven't been rediscovered. When it was a question of publishing the fragments of the 'Angelus' I saw M. Ganderax;[2] undoubtedly he mistrusted my imagination: my account turned into a brief résumé.'

'I would love to hear this résumé.'

'The action begins during the war of 1870, in the environs of Rouen, on the very day that the Prussians invaded the Countess de Brémontal's château. The poor woman had had her father M. Boutemart, Doctor Paturel and the Abbé Marvaux to dinner. The guests have left; her three-year-old son Henri is in bed; she is alone: her husband has been with the army for five months and she is in pain for she is on the verge of giving birth. The enemy arrives. The interview between Mme de Brémontal and the commander of the Prussian detachment is one of extreme intensity. Let's reread this piece, would you like to? The young woman enters, followed by her son:'[3]

***

'You are za lady of zis château?'

The Angelus

[...] Thrown outdoors. So much the better!

***

Mme de Brémontal falls in running away. The poor woman, exhausted, crawls to a stable and, panting, lies down on the straw. The fall has hastened her labour. The same night she brings forth into the world a son who is born, like Christ, in a crib. The poor child is alive, but is the victim of the agonies experienced by his mother during her pregnancy and of the last shock that she had just suffered: his legs are atrophied.

The end of the war arrives. In a last skirmish, M. de Brémontal is killed. The young widow considers her life as over and, bravely, dedicates herself entirely to the education of her two children.

The elder grows up strong and vigorous. Motherly care and attention is not as necessary for him as for the little cripple. Henri is sent to college so as to remove him from the atmosphere of sadness which envelops the house. André grows up but remains unable to stand on his legs. However, if the poor little one's legs stay lifeless, his brain, on the other hand, develops. His mother gives him for teachers the Abbé Marvaux and the son of Doctor Paturel. The characters of these two men were developed in a very interesting way. The abbé represented the most elevated spiritualism, the doctor, on the other hand, a supporter of new ideas, was more disposed to deny than to affirm, but with that was good and charitable, unlike a devotee. In his desire to cure the young de Brémontal, this Doctor Paturel tried desperately and with futility. Obliged to recognize that man's knowledge is, alas, stopped in the face of a certain ineluctable cruelty in nature, and unable to make a strong and sturdy boy of André, he dreams of investing him with a philosophical mind that will help him to understand and bear life.

One day the abbé and the doctor find themselves together in the park of Mme de Brémontal, near the wheelchair in which the young fifteen-year-old invalid lies. The discussion starts off softly. The two interlocutors pay no attention to the child and imperceptibly pass from the most personal of subjects to the most general of ideas:[4]

***

Lecomte du Noüy's account

But thought of Christ haunted the abbé. [...]

'Poor little one, you also, you have received from merciless destiny a sad lot. But you will at least have, I believe, in compensation for all the physical joys, the only beautiful things which have been allowed to men—dream, intelligence and thought.'

***

A few years pass; the finishing touches having been put to the moral education of André, Doctor Paturel sends Mme de Brémontal and her sons to the spas, hoping that this cure will perhaps have a satisfying result; the wise doctor loves his patient too much not to hope for him.

The journey took place. Henri and André settled into the hotel with their mother. Henri, a very adept sportsman, made friends on his arrival with a group of young men and women; they went on trips together and above all played lawn tennis; that's how the young man spent his days.

His brother watched him from his bedroom window. André wasn't happy; the lifestyle at the spas hardly pleased him; the vacuity of the conversations he heard bored him. He appreciated his friends of Rouen far more; he missed their good, serious, and comforting chats.

The patient's unhappiness increased day by day. His mother was anxious. So Henri suggested to André to come and watch the players, but he refused on the pretext that it wasn't his scene.

And so, thanks to a plot hatched by Mme de Brémontal and her elder son, what nobody else could induce André to do, a young girl managed to.

She found some unanswerable arguments and, without further ado, not giving him time to go back on his decision, she pushed the cripple's wheelchair to the tennis and introduced him to her friends. Kindly she strove hard to bring to light the mind of the poor wretch. André's intellectual superiority imposed itself on everyone. Abruptly he felt within him the awakening of life, and his mother thought: 'It's a resurrection!'

One evening, the air is warm, the flowers are fragrant. The unfortunate André converses on the hotel terrace with the young girl. He complains about the sadness

The Angelus

of his kind, of the pain that comes from thinking that never ever will anybody love him.

His companion protests; he listens to her ecstatically. Suddenly he grabs the hand of the young girl and covers it ardently with kisses; surprised by this sudden vigour, she doesn't withdraw her hand, fearful of upsetting the poor patient, and she is far from thinking that he loves her!

So André believes himself loved. The following day, when his mother enters his room, she is surprised to find him better than she's ever seen him: he looks radiant. Mme de Brémontal, for the first time in years, feels almost joyous. Her son Henri has been engaged for a few days, she hasn't yet dared to tell her poor child: on this day she has more courage.

'Who is he marrying?' asks André cheerfully.

'Mlle X…'

It's she whom André loves; the one he thought loved him!

He blacks out. As soon as he comes round he wants to leave, to leave immediately without seeing anyone.

Hardly has the despairing cripple arrived in Rouen when he revolts; he bursts into tears. He reproaches his mother not only with having let him live, but also with having seen to the development of his mind. And he that was born with the first ringing of the angelus in the evening, died with the first sound of the angelus in the morning.

And so the mother, who up until then had remained a fervent Catholic, opened the window in a gesture of sublime insanity, and before the calm beauty of indifferent nature, she burst out in insults and cursed God.

***

[Henri Amic:] 'When I think, my friend, that ten years sufficed for Maupassant to write more than twenty volumes, without counting fragments of novels such as this one; when I think that the brain that engendered a work like 'The Angelus', the mind that conceived these admirable pages on Christ, was on the brink of collapsing irreversibly, I feel myself shiver with fright. Alas! alas! this great injustice happened in order to further add to what Maupassant called: 'The dossier of God'. [5]

Mme de Maupassant's account of *The Angelus* to vicomte de Colleville [1]

At the time of the Prussian invasion, a Frenchwoman, already the mother of a son, finds herself pregnant. Whilst fleeing from the enemy, the poor woman has a fall, and the child that she is carrying comes into the world crippled and frail; but the little cripple soon shows such a lively and charming intelligence that the deformity of his body is almost forgotten. To this boy deprived of life the mother shows a tenderness still more exquisite than for the other child. She prefers him so much to the elder that any happiness that befalls the firstborn seems to her unjustly stolen from the second born. And so they grow up and, having reached manhood, they both meet a young girl with whom they fall in love at the same time. At first, equally liking both boys, the girl suddenly becomes more reserved towards the elder, because he is handsome and she loves him; on the other hand, she appears more affectionately familiar, more tender even towards the cripple, for whom she holds only feelings of friendship, pointless to disguise. The poor boy imagines that he is loved, and an inexpressible joy floods this soul, that up until then had been so painfully sombre, with a heavenly ray.

The awakening is cruel, the older brother asks for and obtains the hand of the young girl, and when reality brutally explodes in front of the cripple's eyes, he falls from such a height that he is shattered, struck down. A burning fever seizes hold of him and, in his delirium, he always sees his beloved in the arms of the preferred rival. Up until then Christian and pious, the mother, now despairing, feels well up within the depth of her being revolt and anger against the heaven that unrelentingly

The Angelus

works at martyrizing her youngest son. However the illness grows worse: it's evening, in a Norman manor, the mother sits up with the child who suffers still more and, in his sleep, he utters words rapidly; the mother draws near and listens: it's the name of the adored girl which the invalid repeats passionately. At this very moment, slowly, in the twilight, grows the ringing of the *Angelus*. And unconsciously, with her usual religiosity, the mother bends her knees and crosses herself according to custom; but suddenly she remembered, she turns around and, embracing the body of her son with a stricken look, trembling, she gets up, and stinging heaven with superb imprecations, she insults this God who feeds himself on tears and takes pleasure in the sufferings of his creatures.

All these details that I give to you on Guy de Maupassant I have drawn from a source exclusive to me, I have them from his very mother, who, because of an old family friendship wanted to bestow on me the great honour of giving them to me.

Vicomte de Colleville.

Mme de Maupassant's account of *The Angelus* to Mademoiselle Ray and Dr Balestre [1]

His last novel, *The Angelus*, had been recounted by him to Mme de Maupassant, who piously remembers the work that no one will ever know in its entirety.

At Aix-les-Bains,[2] Guy was walking one evening with his mother. A reverent silence reigned in the fragrant shadows and he found his denouement.

It was the heroine's cursing of a fierce God who, beneath men, had made a crucified son and a grieving mother, the apotheosis of suffering.

This apostrophe faded in the sombre air like a storm of genius which, for a moment, glorified the landscape then never materialized.

Guy, in order to write this *Angelus*, had interrupted *The Foreign Soul*, of which the *Revue de Paris* has also published fragments. He abandoned the first work not through caprice—his mind was too disciplined to waver between two inspirations—but because the heroine was Romanian and he wanted to live in the same environment as her. And he had resolved to accept the invitation of Carmen-Sylva to spend a few weeks at her court.[3]

François Tassart's account of *The Angelus*[1]

After having cast an eye over the palais des Papes, we cross the Rhône and visit the ancient town of Villeneuve-d'Avignon.[2] We return to Avignon, after having crossed again the river which flows majestically and that is seen snaking into the distance from the height of the bridge. On a terrace to the left which overlooks the square and the palais des Papes, we noticed a large chapel, Notre-Dame des Doms.[3] My master says to me: 'Let's have a little look; sometimes there are old monuments inside, things to be examined up close, such as stained glass windows, etc…' After having made a tour of the church we noticed to the left, near the entrance, a hall, and there, in a glass reliquary, a saint of natural grandeur was lain out. Monsieur looks at it with a great deal of attention, as he does all things which he wants to study thoroughly and in a loud voice he says: 'This statue is the work of an Italian artist. In France we don't know how to achieve such an artistic finish.' On leaving he gave some change to the woman who was in charge of the holy water. From her he learns that the pretty saint that he had just been admiring, Nevia-Félicité, had been given to this church by Pope Pius IX.[4]

Going back to the station, Monsieur gave looks to left and to right down narrow streets where the façades of gothic monuments were seen. In the evening, he announces to me that we can leave for Nîmes,[5] and he adds: 'It will be amusing later, when M. Dumas[6] asks me where I got my woman's face from, and I answer him: "From a reliquary in Notre-Dames des Doms of Avignon…" It's true to say that I haven't found in that face everything I need for my female character. However, I saw there, in the expression of the face, the rough diamond that I will cut; I made out in it the artistic details that will serve me in forming the contours of my subject, that I hope to succeed in rendering in a striking manner, closely touching perfection. I am going to, what's more, in my *Angelus*, use the full power of expression of which I'm capable; much care will be taken over all the details within it, with a meticulousness that nothing will weary. I feel admirably situated to do this book, which I know inside out so well and that I have conceived with a surprising ease. It will be the crowning of my literary career, I am convinced that its qualities will fill the artistic reader with such enthusiasm that he'll wonder whether he finds himself looking at reality or a novel...'

Appendix

Appendix—Manuscript Variants in *The Angelus*

In the Conard edition, that is, *Oeuvres posthumes*, vol. II, ed. Pol Neveux (Paris: Louis Conard, 1910), five pages of the manuscript of *The Angelus* were reproduced in facsimile: pp. 1, 8, and 23 of ch. I; p. 3 of Fragment III; and Fragment IV. Some of the variant readings from these manuscript pages have been transcribed in the notes of *Romans*, ed. Louis Forestier (Paris: Gallimard 'Bibliothèque de la Pléiade', 1987), pp. 1685-8; and *Boule de suif et autres histoires de guerre*, ed. Antonia Fonyi (Paris: Flammarion, 1991), pp. 293-5. I have used these transcriptions of folios 1, 8, and 23 of ch. I in my translation of the variants below (Forestier and Fonyi don't give readings of folio 3 of Fragment III and Fragment IV, the manuscript being heavy with illegible crossings out—the few that I give are my own readings). Words that were crossed out are recorded in ~~strikethrough~~; words added appear in curly brackets { }; my editorial clarifications are in square brackets [ ], giving the original French words in *italics*. Page numbers and line numbers refer to the text of the English translation in this volume.

From folio 1 of ch. I of MS; p. 41 English text

l. 1
The clock struck ~~seven~~ {six} and

ll. 2-3
looked up ~~at the fireplace of her large~~ {at the dial of the handsome [Louis XVI] wall clock} {~~suspended~~ [*pend*]} {hung [*accroché*]} {~~from the high wall~~ [*à la muraille*]}

The Angelus

{upon the wall [*sur le mur*]}; then

l. 5
A ~~large~~ {~~handsome~~} {~~ch~~[*arbon* = coal?]} {log} fire, flaming

l. 6
threw ~~a large~~ a broken glimmer

ll. 6-7
lighting up {the characters on the tapestries}, the gold frames

ll. 8-9
the high curtains that {draped and} veiled the windows in a ~~red black~~ {dark red} light ~~and the doors~~. In spite of ~~all~~ [*tous*] {all [*toutes*]} these ~~fires~~ {lights} the ~~large~~ vast

ll. 10-11
the air ~~and~~ and the breath of the ~~frozen~~ wind ~~which ran across the ground snow~~ {frozen by the carpet of snow stretched out over the earth and} making the trees ~~and~~ in the park ~~groan~~ {creak}.

l. 12
The countess rose; ~~and~~

ll. 12-13
slightly slow, ~~heavy~~ {shuffling} gait of a young ~~six months~~ pregnant woman

ll. 14-16
~~The emanation of heat from the~~ {The} blazing logs ~~covered her with a burning caress whilst the~~ threw on them the emanation of their lively heat, a kind of burning, {even} slightly brutal, caress, whilst {at the same time} she felt her back ~~and~~, shoulders and neck {continue to} shiver ~~from~~ [*du*] {with [*sous*]} the frisson

Appendix—Manuscript Variants in The Angelus

From folio 8 of ch. I of MS; p. 46 English text

ll. 4-5
If it wasn't for this {rule} {which they} always ~~respect~~ {observe}, I would've

ll. 11-12
~~He replied, u~~ {U}nderstanding in truth that it was ~~im to~~ [im de] impossible to leave his daughter alone in the face of this {terrible and} immanent threat

l. 14
'~~Well, listen~~ {All the same,} you are right. There

ll. 15-16
I will ~~leave for~~ return to Dieppedalle

From folio 23 of ch. I of MS; p. 54 English text

ll. 1-2
her tastes, her ~~tender~~ ideal of woman.

l. 4
this ~~impossible~~ ungraspable dream, ~~and~~ addressed

l. 8
ardent believer, {having been} brought up

ll. 9-10
Mme Boutemart, in effect, born ~~in~~ [aux] {in} [à] the era

l. 11
the Revolution had made ~~faith~~ {pious beliefs} disappear

ll. 12-14
that her father ~~a former soldier of the Republic then the Empire,~~ had inculcated

The Angelus

her with.
   {Her daughter} Germaine

l. 15
she received from her mother ~~nothing~~ no further ~~of~~ doctrine

ll. 16-17
elegant Paris boarding school ~~in order to there~~ {where she} complete{d} her education

Folio 3 of Fragment III of MS; p. 64 English text

ll. 21-2
   {The doctor riposted:}
   'Monsieur ~~l'abbé~~ {le curé}

ll. 26-7
the wrongdoings of ~~God~~ Providence.

l. 29
You too, moreover{, who cares for their souls}.

l. 33
'We can ~~never do anything~~ do nothing to penetrate

l. 34
Personally, ~~must one~~ I don't ~~know~~ {believe} that ~~I understand~~ [*je comprends*] {I can understand [*je comprenne*]} God.

Folio 3 of Fragment III of MS; p. 65 English text

ll. 12-13
O lord crucified on ~~the cross~~ {the Calvary}

Appendix—Manuscript Variants in The Angelus

From Fragment IV of MS; English text p. 67

l. 1
> ~~Murder~~
> ~~We are unhinged~~ [*Désaxons?*]
> {Eternal} Murderer ~~eternal~~

ll. 1-3
the pleasure of creating in order to ~~taste the tireless~~ {savour tirelessly his {relentless} passion} of killing {anew}, of beginning again his

Notes

Notes

The Foreign Soul

Chapter One

[1] The casino at Aix-les-Bains, known as the Grand Cercle, was founded in 1824 in rooms that were part of the château of the marquis d'Aix. Construction on new buildings designed by the architect Bernard Pellegrini began in 1847 opening in 1849, including concert and ballrooms, reading and drawing rooms, and a 700-capacity theatre that opened in 1853. The construction of a new theatre at the Grand Cercle began in 1885, it was built by H Eustache with a capacity for 1000; the old theatre was turned into a concert hall. Henri Meilhac (1831-97), was a French dramatist and librettist, elected to the Académie française in 1888. The comedy might be one of *Décoré* (1888), *Pepa* (1888), *Margot* (1890), or *Ma cousine* (1890). Maupassant attended the first production of *Pepa* which debuted at the Comédie-Française, in Paris, October 31, 1888 (see Maupassant's telegram to Henry Cazalis, October 27, 1888, in *Correspondance*, ed. Jacques Suffel, 3 vols. (Geneva: Edito Service, 1973), vol. III, letter no. 534).

[2] Casinos ran on a membership basis. Douglas Peter Mackaman describes the sense of exclusivity this system cultivated in *Leisure Settings: Bourgeois Culture, Medicine, and the Spa in Modern France* (Chicago and London: The University of Chicago Press, 1998), ch. 5 'Social Benefits of Spa Consumption', pp. 132-3:

> Keeping the "wrong" people out of a spa casino, however, was hardly a military or police matter. Rather, an apparently strict bureaucratic screening, details of which were clearly posted throughout the *villes d'eaux* and carefully described in virtually every guidebook, saw more effectively to the controlling of these institutions' constituencies. Curists, in fact, had to join

a casino—whose management usually reported to a profit-sensitive corporation—before they could use any of its facilities. Daily memberships were by far the most common way to join a casino. For a membership of this type, all one had to do was pay the casino's admission charge of several francs.

Joining a casino for the duration of one's vacation, which only 15 to 20 percent of a spa's visiting population ever did, was, however, a significantly more complicated affair. Hopeful members had to first present letters of reference and nomination to a casino's governing body, upon whose review and recommendation all admissions depended. Merely a formality for upper bourgeois spa-goers, as were the seasonal dues of twenty-five francs per person, this presentation of credentials doubtlessly caused a certain measure of trepidation among some middle-class initiates. Notwithstanding the fact that administrative scrutiny seldom if ever barred an interested middle bourgeois from partaking in a casino's charms, there can be little doubt that such membership policies conferred status—by offering a very public validation of one's social credentials—onto those who elected to join a casino as full members.

3 Louis d'or—any of several gold coins introduced by Louis XIII (1601-43, r. 1610-43) in 1640; after the French Revolution it was the name of a 20 fr. gold coin.

4 In French *smoking*, a word that had only recently entered the language; for more on the tuxedo see n. 10 below.

5 In French 'dans une tête de fille, et de fille de concierge'. The French word *fille* can be translated as 'girl', 'daughter', or 'whore' and will hereafter be given in square brackets within the text, allowing the reader to either agree or baulk in disgust at my rendering.

6 An alternate draft of the following conversation is given on pp. 19-23.

7 A député is a member of the Chambre des Députés, the legislative assembly of French parliament; *the Union of Industrial Towns [l'Union des villes industrielles]* is fictional.

8 The avenue Montaigne is a street in the 8th arrondissement of Paris, in Maupassant's day it was nicknamed the 'avenue des Veuves [widowers]' and was renowned for its hotels and opulent houses, today it is famed for its fashion stores.

9 The Palais de l'Industrie was an exhibition hall built for the Paris World's Fair in 1855 located between the Seine and the Champs-Élysées, designed by Jean-Marie Victor Viel (1796-1863) and Alexandre Barrault (1812-65), it served as a venue for numerous exhibitions until its destruction in 1897, including the Salon annuel de peinture which opened each year on the first of May.

Notes

¹⁰ The tuxedo was invented by Henry Poole & Co. in 1860 as a smoking jacket for the Prince of Wales, the future Edward VII (1841-1910; r. 1901-10).

¹¹ Maupassant uses the English word 'gentlemen'.

¹² The Académie française is the official authority on the French language and was founded in 1635 by Cardinal Richelieu (1585-1642), one of its major roles being to publish the official dictionary, the *Dictionnaire de l'Académie française*. The Académie is made up of 40 members known as *immortels* [immortals] who hold their seats for life; vacant seats are filled by election by the other members. The Académie issues numerous annual prizes; prizes for history that had been established in the nineteenth century included the Grand Prix Gobert (est. 1834, awarded annually), the Prix Thiers (est. 1862, awarded triennially), and the Prix Thérouanne (est. 1869, awarded annually).

¹³ Chambotte is a village 15 km north of Aix-les-Bains, on the mountain La Chambotte, 3000 ft high; it was a popular destination for excursions from Aix as it provided a fine panoramic view overlooking the lac du Bourget.

¹⁴ The Hôtel des Souverains is fictional.

¹⁵ The italicized phrase is in English (and italics) in the original.

¹⁶ Maupassant uses the English word 'high-life'.

Chapter Two

¹ Douglas Peter Mackaman describes these sedan chairs in *Leisure Settings*, ch. 4, 'Medicine and the Rhythming of Bourgeois Rest', p. 87: 'The bath or sedan chair was little more than a boxed-in seat mounted on two carrying poles. This simple mode of conveyance, which brought so many bathers from their hotels to a spa and then back again, was identified by guidebook authors as an experience that bespoke the spas' new commitment to privacy'. The chairs were seemingly used not just for reasons of modesty, but also health, preventing chills (ibid., p. 118).

François Tassart's account of research for *The Foreign Soul*

¹ Translated from François Tassart (1856-1949), *Souvenirs sur Guy de Maupassant par François son valet de chambre (1883-1893)* (Paris: Plon-Nourrit et Cie, 1911), ch. XV, pp. 230-4.

² The Hôtel de l'Europe was found on the rue du Casino.

³ Le Revard or Mont Revard (1545 m) is 10 km by rail east of Aix, offering superb views of Mont Blanc and the lac du Bourget; it is now popular for winter sports.

Notes

⁴ The Dent du Chat (5000 ft) is the highest peak of the Mont du Chat, a mountain whose name has had several origins attributed it: that the rocks on its summit look like a cat; that a large savage feline terrorized the locality until it was killed in the 6th century; or that it is derived from the word *Caturgies*, the name by which the primitive inhabitants of the area were known. The lac du Bourget is found 7.5 km west of Aix, it is 18 km long and up to 145 m deep in places, it empties into the Rhône and provided sources of amusement to visitors of Aix with sailing, boating, swimming, fishing and searching for relics of the ancient lacustrines popular activities.

⁵ The Villa des Fleurs was a casino that was established in 1880 in the grounds of a beautiful park; in the early twentieth century it combined its entrance fees with the Grand Cercle.

⁶ Eugénia María de Montijo de Guzmán (1826-1920), Eugénie, the Spanish empress of France (1853-70), the wife of Napoléon III (1808-73, emperor of France 1852-70).

⁷ Petits chevaux was a popular game of chance, similar to roulette, played at casinos in the nineteenth and early twentieth centuries. People would place stakes on nine differently coloured mechanical horses that revolved in concentric circles around a central axis, the winner being the closest to a given mark.

⁸ *lèse-amour*, lit. meaning 'an affront to love', and coined in the fashion of the word *lèse-majesté*.

⁹ Bernard and Raymond, two brothers-in-law, were skipper and first mate respectively on Maupassant's yacht *Bel-Ami*, appearing in Maupassant's travel book *Sur l'eau* (1888) translated as *Afloat*, by Marlo Johnston (London: Peter Owen, 1995).

¹⁰ Marlioz-les-Bains, 2 km south of Aix, had its own thermal establishment; the road linking it to Aix was the avenue de Marlioz.

¹¹ Valence is the capital of the Drôme département (no. 26) about 65 miles south of Lyons. It is on the railway line to Marseille and now has a lavishly designed TGV station, the Gare de Valence TGV. Grenoble is capital of the Isère département (no. 38) and is nicknamed 'the capital of the Alps' by the French.

François Tassart's account of Alexandre Dumas fils' involvement with *The Foreign Soul*

¹ Translated from François Tassart, *Nouveaux souvenirs intimes sur Guy de Maupassant (inédits)*, ed. Pierre Cogny (Paris: A G Nizet, 1962), ch. XVII 'Souvenirs d'Étretat' (written in Paris, 1921), pp. 162-6.

Notes

² Marie-Angèle Séon (1835-1914), wife of Alexis Pasquier, otherwise known as Pasca, was an esteemed actress and friend of Gustave Flaubert.
³ Alexandre Dumas fils (1824-95), French novelist and dramatist.
⁴ Aristotle (384-322 BC), Greek philosopher, was the first person in Western literature to mention silk and its manufacture, in his *History of Animals*, tr. Richard Cresswell (London: Henry G Bohn, 1862), pp. 124-5:

> A certain great worm, which has as it were horns, and differs from others, at its first metamorphosis produces a campe [caterpillar], afterwards a bombylius, and lastly a necydalus [chrysalis]. It passes through all these forms in six months. From this animal some women unroll and separate the bombycina (cocoons), and afterwards weave them. It is said that this was first woven in the island of Cos by Pamphila, the daughter of Plateos.

⁵ George Sand (pseud. Amandine-Aurore Lucille Dupin, Baronne Dudevant, 1804-76), French novelist.
⁶ Gustave Flaubert (1821-80), French writer whose novel *Madame Bovary* was serialized in the *Revue de Paris* in 1856 before being published in book form in 1857 (Paris: Michel Lévy Frères). Flaubert, who had been a childhood friend of Maupassant's mother, was an avuncular figure for Maupassant, encouraging, supporting and aiding him in his literary endeavours, and also his life in general. It was Flaubert who secured Maupassant's transfer from the Ministry of the Marine and Colonies to a more comfortable position at the Ministry of Education and it was to Flaubert that Maupassant turned when faced with a charge of 'outrage against decency and public morality' for the publication of his poem 'Une Fille' in November 1879. A letter from Flaubert, printed in *Le Gaulois*, helped get charges dropped. Maupassant was devastated by Flaubert's death and indeed honoured and cherished their friendship for the rest of his own life. Maupassant was perhaps more than anyone else Flaubert's literary disciple and heir, following and preaching his advice and dictates (see Maupassant's essay 'Le Roman' ['The Novel'] which prefaces *Pierre et Jean* (1888)) and honouring his literary master with the success he achieved by applying these methods. Maupassant also wrote several articles on Flaubert after his death and throughout the following decade: 'Souvenirs d'un an. Un après-midi chez Gustave Flaubert', in *Le Gaulois*, August 23, 1880; 'Gustave Flaubert d'après ses lettres', in *Le Gaulois*, September 6, 1880; 'Gustave Flaubert dans sa vie intime', in *La Nouvelle Revue*, January 1, 1881; 'Bouvard et

Pécuchet', in *Supplément du Gaulois*, April 6, 1881; 'Gustave Flaubert', in *Revue Bleue*, January 19 and 25, 1884 and as a preface to *Lettres de Gustave Flaubert à George Sand* (Paris: Charpentier, 1884); 'Gustave Flaubert', in *L'Écho de Paris*, November 24, 1890; and 'Flaubert et sa maison', in the supplement of *Gil Blas*, November 24, 1890.

[7] The 1848 French Revolution saw the abdication of King Louis-Philippe (1773-1850, r. 1830-1848) on February 24 with the Second Republic being proclaimed two days later on February 26. The Second Republic was short-lived (1848-51), and its first two years were fraught with political upheaval and instability as liberals, conservatives and left-wing radicals sought power and reform. Universal male suffrage was introduced along with taxes on landowners to help alleviate urban unemployment. These taxes were unpopular and largely ignored losing the Provisional Government of the newly drawn up Constituent Assembly the support of the rural majority. The Constituent Assembly's decision to close National Workshops (formed to provide work for the unemployed) on June 21, 1848, led to the 'June Days Uprising' of 23-25 June, where a working-class revolt was crushed brutally by the War Minister, General Louis Cavaignac (1802-57), with 1,500 people killed and thousands of arrests. Cavaignac was appointed head of state before a new constitution was drawn up in December and Louis Napoléon Bonaparte (1808-73, President of Second Republic 1848-52, emperor of France as Napoléon III 1852-70) was elected as President. By 1850, as Dumas indicates, the situation was more stable, but the government had moved more and more to the right after the Constituent Assembly was dissolved in May 1849 and a new Legislative Assembly elected.

[8] Michel Martin Drolling (1786-1851), French painter, elected to the Académie des Beaux-Arts in 1837. Drolling's painting *Jésus au milieu des docteurs* (1836) hangs in the choir of the church of Notre-Dame de Lorette on the rue de Châteaudun, Paris.

[9] [Note by François Tassart] By secret means, M. Dumas obtained the liberation of this lady, but could never see her again.

[10] Ostend oysters, smaller than common oysters, are actually British in origin, exported to Belgium to be grown in artificial beds in the English Channel. They were a much esteemed delicacy in Paris and Maupassant describes them in *Bel-Ami*, tr. Douglas Parmée (Harmondsworth: Penguin, 1975), ch. 5, p. 105: 'Succulent Ostend oysters were brought in, looking like dainty little ears enclosed in shells and melting between the tongue and the palate like salty tidbits.' The town of Nazareth in Israel is situated in a particularly fertile valley, 'it is filled with corn-fields, with gardens, hedges of

cactus, and clusters of fruit-bearing trees. Being so sheltered by hills, Nazareth enjoys a mild atmosphere and climate. Hence all the fruits of the country—as pomegranates, oranges, figs, olives,—ripen early and retain a rare perfection.' (William Smith, *A Dictionary of the Bible* (Boston: Little, Brown, and Company, 1863), vol. II, p. 469.)

[11] Maupassant's 'Au bord de l'eau' first appeared under the pseudonym of Guy de Valmont in the French Jewish poet Catulle Mendès' (1841-1909) magazine *République des Lettres*, March 20, 1876. It was reprinted, in a slightly abridged form, under the title of 'Une Fille', in the *Revue moderne et naturaliste*, November 1, 1879. Describing a short-lived passionate physical affair between the narrator and a washerwoman, the public prosecutors of Étampes, the town in which *Revue moderne et naturaliste* was published, thought that the erotic content of 'Une fille' was an 'outrage against decency and public morality' and brought charges against both Maupassant and the publication's editor, Harry Alis (pseud. Hippolyte Percher, 1857-95)—the real target of the magistrates' wrath for his anti-establishment criticisms in the *Revue moderne et naturaliste* and his other paper, *L'Abeille*. Maupassant began to fear for his job at the Ministry of Education and turned to Gustave Flaubert, who had faced similar charges against *Madame Bovary* in 1857, for support and advice. A letter of defence from Flaubert, printed in *Le Gaulois*, February 21, combined with the fact that the poem had already appeared three years earlier without censure meant that the prosecution was dropped by February 27. Maupassant included 'Au bord de l'eau' in his collection *Des Vers* (Paris: Charpentier, 1880), that appeared just a couple of months later in May.

[12] In the French the word is only partially given, 'co...', I have taken this to be *cocu*, 'cuckold'.

[13] Maupassant never wrote a work with this title.

[14] The Crimean War (March 1854-February 1856) between an alliance of Britain, France and Sardinia on one side and the Russian Empire on the other.

[15] Double boots have an outer shell with an inner removable lining.

[16] [Note by François Tassart] Now that the preceding facts belong to history, here are the names:
Général Narechkine [more commonly spelled 'Narishkin'—JW], minister, and Mme la Générale, née Sareste were, along with M. Alexandre Dumas fils, the real characters in this tragedy.

Notes

Paul Bourget 'An Unfinished Novel by Maupassant'

1   Paul Bourget (1852-1935), French novelist and critic; 'An Unfinished Novel by Maupassant' ['Un Roman Inachevé de Maupassant'] is taken from Bourget's book, *Nouvelles Pages de Critique et de Doctrine* (Paris: Plon-Nourrit et Cie, 1922), vol. I, pt. I, ch. V, pp. 65-74.

2   Guy de Maupassant, *The Foreign Soul*, p. 3 herein; there may be a typo or slight misquotation of Maupassant in Bourget's essay as he gives 'd'une source de louis roulant [rolling] sur les quatre tapis' whereas all the editions of the text of *L'Ame étrangère* that I have consulted give 'd'une source de louis coulant [flowing] sur les quatre tapis'.

3   The *Revue de Paris*, November 15, 1894, in which *L'Ame étrangère* was first published.

4   Benozzo Gozzoli (c. 1421-97), Florentine artist. Between 1469 and 1485 Gozzoli painted the series of frescos depicting Old Testament scenes on the Campo Santo (a walled cemetery) in Pisa—many of which were destroyed in an air attack by Allied bombers in 1944, making Bourget's description of them as 'dying' and 'devoured by time' sound all the more ominous. Domenico Ghirlandaio (1449-94), Florentine painter. The choir of the church of Santa Maria Novella in Florence contains a series of frescos depicting scenes from the lives of the Virgin Mary and John the Baptist painted between 1485-90 by Ghirlandaio, who was assisted by his young apprentice Michelangelo Buonarroti (1475-1564). Leonardo da Vinci (1452-1519), Florentine artist, scientist, inventor and writer. Da Vinci's fresco *The Last Supper* (1495-8) was painted on to the back wall of the refectory at the church of Santa Maria delle Grazie in Milan.

5   Cf. Georges Normandy, *La Fin de Maupassant* (Paris: Albin Michel, 1927), p. 202, where Maupassant is said to have claimed: 'Mon manuscrit que je voulais détruire a été volé par le diable...' ['My manuscript that I wanted to destroy has been stolen by the devil...'—All translations are mine unless stated otherwise]. Maupassant had previously asked his valet, François Tassart, to burn his manuscripts (ibid., p. 200). Maupassant's manuscript may indeed have been 'stolen' from him, on his mother's orders—she was worried that her son would want to destroy his manuscripts, their content not in accord with the rather ecstatic religious state of mind that he had entered into whilst a resident of Dr Blanche's clinic in Passy, and asked for them to be safeguarded (see Laure de Maupassant's letter, ibid., pp. 195-8).

6   *L'Angélus* was published in the *Revue de Paris*, April 1, 1895.

Notes

[7] 'Boule de suif' is probably Maupassant's most famous story and marked his literary breakthrough when it was first published on April 17, 1880 in *Les Soirées de Médan* (Paris: Charpentier), a collection of stories by the Naturalist school of writers that had gathered around Émile Zola (1840-92), meeting at his home in the village of Médan. *Les Soirées de Médan* took as its theme the Franco-Prussian War (1870-1), the other stories in the volume were: 'L'Attaque du Moulin' by Zola; 'Après la bataille' by Paul Alexis (1847-1901); 'Sac au dos' by Joris-Karl Huysmans (1848-1907); 'L'Affaire du Grand 7' by Léon Hennique (1851-1935); and 'Une saignée' by Henry Céard (1851-1924).

[8] Honoré de Balzac (1799-1850), French writer; Prosper Mérimée (1803-70), French playwright and short story writer; and Ivan Turgenev (1818-83), Russian writer and friend of Maupassant.

[9] Hippolyte Taine (1828-93), French philosopher, historian and critic. Taine's *De l'Intelligence* [*On Intelligence*], 2 vols. (Paris: Hachette, 1870) was an influential work of psychology and philosophy.

[10] Guy de Maupassant, *The Foreign Soul*, p. 3 herein.

[11] Jean de La Bruyère (1645-96), French writer; Stendhal (pseud. Marie Henri Beyle 1783-1842), French writer.

[12] Flaubert, Letter to Louise Colet, December 9, 1852, which can be found in *Correspondance*, 13 vols. (Paris: Conard, 1926-33, 1954), vol. 3, pp. 61-2.

[13] Bourget here writes 'les génératrices', using the word as a substantive. As a noun *génératrice* has a number of scientific and technical meanings, primarily that of a 'generator' or 'dynamo' in electronics and mechanics and a 'generator' or 'generatrix' in mathematics. However, as far as I can tell, Taine uses *générateur / génératrice* as an adjective, to be translated as 'generative'.

[14] In French 'à hauteur d'appui', lit. 'at elbow *or* leaning height'.

[15] Maupassant published *Pierre et Jean* (Paris: Ollendorff) on January 9, 1888, after it had been serialized in *La Nouvelle Revue* in the issues of December 1 and 15, 1887 and January 1, 1888.

[16] Maupassant published *Notre coeur* in *La Revue des Deux Mondes*, in the issues of May 15, June 1 and 15, 1890, followed in June by publication in book form (Paris: Ollendorff). *Notre coeur* was not in fact the last published work by Maupassant—he had a handful of articles appear in periodicals later in 1890 and 1891, whilst his play *Musotte* written with Jacques Normand, was performed and published in 1891 (Paris: Ollendorff).

[17] Pierre Loti (pseud. Louis Marie-Julien Viaud 1850-1923), French writer whose works were famed for their exoticism. *Pêcheur d'Islande* (Paris: Calmann-Lévy, 1886), translated into English as *The Iceland Fisherman*, was a novel about life among the fishermen of Brittany who sailed north each year to fish off the waters of Iceland. In *Pêcheur d'Islande* Loti sought to adapt some of the techniques of the Impressionist painters to French prose, resulting in some wonderful descriptions of nature.

[18] In the French 'le conflit des races'—Bourget is probably taking the lead from Maupassant's title, *The Foreign Soul*, in using the word *race* and is primarily talking about the battle of the sexes; but that he is also pointing out difference in race or nationality is supported by what Bourget says in a later essay, named after Maupassant's novel, 'L'Ame Étrangère', in *Nouvelles Pages de Critique et de Doctrine*, vol. II, pt. III, ch. IV, p. 47:

> *L'Ame étrangère*,—ainsi s'appelait, on s'en souvient, le roman auquel travaillait Maupassant quand la maladie, dont il devait mourir, lui arracha la plume des mains. Les morceaux inachevés de ce livre nous permettent de discerner nettement son intention. Il voulait montrer la réciproque inintelligibilité de deux amants issus de deux pays différents, et que travaillent des nationalités, irréductibles l'une à l'autre, même par la passion et par la tendresse.

> [*The Foreign Soul*—so is named the novel, if you can remember, on which Maupassant was working when the illness from which he would die wrested the pen from his hands. The unfinished pieces of this book allow us to discern clearly his intention. He wanted to show the reciprocal unintelligibility of two lovers coming from two different countries who are tormented by each other's insurmountable nationalities, even through passion and tenderness.]

[19] Maupassant published *Mont-Oriol* (Paris: Victor Havard) in February 1887, after it had been serialized in *Gil Blas* from December 23, 1886 to February 6, 1887.

[20] Fernand Xau (1852-99) founded *Le Journal*, a daily Paris newspaper, in 1892 intending it to be a literary journal devoid of politics and aimed at readers not targeted by other literary papers, especially women and men from the lower social classes. Xau edited *Le Journal* until his death in 1899. Henri Léon Emile Lavedan (1859-1940), French writer and one of *Le Journal*'s journalists.

Notes

[21] The marble bust of Maupassant by sculptor Raoul Verlet (1857-1923) and architect Henri Deglane (1855-1931) was unveiled on October 24, 1897 in the parc Monceau, in the 8th arrondissement of Paris.

[22] In the Jardin du Luxembourg, the largest public park in Paris and situated in the 6th arrondissement, there is a bronze bust of Stendhal, by the French sculptor Auguste Rodin (1840-1917) from the medallion of another French sculptor, Pierre-Jean David d'Angers (1788-1856). The bust of Stendhal decorates a large monument that was inaugurated on June 28, 1920. The Jardin du Luxembourg also sports a statue of George Sand (1905) by the French sculptor François-Léon Sicard (1862-1934), and a stone bust of Flaubert by French sculptor Jean-Baptiste (known as Auguste) Clésinger (1814-83) inaugurated in 1921 for the centenary of Flaubert's birth.

[23] Balzac's lavishly decorated house, nicknamed 'la Folie Beaujon' (after Nicolas Beaujon (1718-86), the wealthy French banker who had the original palace built, of which Balzac's residence was the remaining part), no. 22 rue Fortunée (now called rue Balzac), which he bought in 1846, dying there in 1850, was purchased by the Baroness Adèle de Rothschild (1843-1922) in 1882 and demolished before the century was out as the baroness incorporated the land into her gardens. Balzac's house at no. 1 rue Cassini, where he lived from 1828-36, was demolished in 1897. After the death of Balzac's wife, Eveline, on April 11, 1882, his possessions from the rue Fortunée, including his manuscripts, were either seized by creditors or hastily auctioned off.

[24] Alfred de Musset (1810-57), French writer who died of a rare heart condition on May 2, 1857 and was buried two days later at Père Lachaise cemetery in Paris on May 4.

[25] Jules Amédée Barbey d'Aurevilly (1808-89), French writer who in spite of poverty was known for his dandyism.

[26] Jean-Jacques Weiss (1827-91), French literary critic, scholar and journalist.

[27] Hippolyte Taine received the Légion d'honneur in 1866. The Légion d'honneur, established in 1802, is the highest honour in France and is divided into five degrees: Chevalier, Officier, Commandeur, Grand Officier, and Grand-Croix, with Chevalier being the lowest rank and Grand-Croix of the highest merit.

The Angelus

Chapter One

[1] The manuscript of ch. I of *The Angelus* consists of thirty-four pages numbered 1-34,

the last of which consisting of fifteen lines. Five pages of the manuscript of *The Angelus* were reproduced in facsimile in the Conard edition, including pages no. 1, 8, and 23 of ch. I; variant readings from these five pages are given in the Appendix.

² The coupé was a light four-wheeled closed carriage that could be pulled by one, two or four horses. The driver would sit on a box seat outside at the front whilst inside would seat two (sometimes with an additional fold away seat).

³ La Bouille is a village on the south bank of the river Seine about 12 miles downstream from Rouen, in the Seine-Maritime département (no. 76). The village still has a ferry, le Bac, which connects La Bouille to Sahurs on the other bank. Now motorized, the ferry was formerly a 30 ft long shallow-draft boat commanded by two ferrymen using long oars from standing positions, whilst there were two rowing boats for foot passengers operated by a single oarsman each.

⁴ The last verse of Victor Hugo's 'La fête chez Thérèse' ['Thérèse's Party'] from his volume *Les contemplations* (1856).

⁵ On December 4, 1870, French troops guarding Rouen were driven back in a skirmish with the Prussians and General Guillaume Briand (1815-94), head of the 2nd Military Division, decided to withdraw the French forces to Le Havre. The VIII (Rhineland) army corps, led by August Karl von Goeben (1816-80), part of the I army commanded by Edwin Freiherr von Manteuffel (1809-95), entered Rouen unopposed on December 5.

⁶ Pont-Audemur is a town on the banks of the river Risle, about 30 miles west of Rouen, in the Eure département (no. 27).

⁷ Honfleur is a picturesque port located on the southern banks of the Seine estuary in the Calvados département (no. 14).

⁸ Dieppedalle is a village on the outskirts of Rouen on the north bank of the Seine, in the Seine-Maritime département (no. 76).

⁹ In 1859 Napoléon III helped the Sardinian monarchy expel the Austrians from Lombardy in the Second Italian War of Independence.

¹⁰ La place de l'Hôtel de Ville is at the centre of the old town part of Rouen, dominated by the Gothic church of l'abbatiale Saint-Ouen, and the Hôtel de Ville [town hall] which adjoins it. Maupassant gives a slightly more detailed description of the Prussians' arrival in Rouen in 'Boule de suif', in *Selected Short Stories*, tr. Roger Colet (Harmondsworth: Penguin, 1971), p. 21:

Notes

On the afternoon of the day following the departure of the French troops, a few Uhlans, appearing from heaven knows where, galloped through the town. Then, a little later, a dark mass of troops swept down St Catherine's hill, while two other invading torrents streamed in along the roads from Darnetal and Boisguillaume. The advance-guards of the three bodies, arriving at exactly the same moment, linked up on the Place del'Hôtel-de-Ville; and the German army came pouring down all the nearby streets, the cobblestones ringing under the heavy, measured tread of its battalions.

[11] Bourg-Achard is a village about twenty km downstream from Rouen, in the Eure département (no. 27).

[12] As in the English, the French *fortune* can mean both luck and wealth.

[13] Louis Léon César Faidherbe (1818-89), French colonial administrator and general. Having been governor of the French colony of Senegal (1854-61, 1863-5) and then a commander in the Constantine province of Algeria, Faidherbe was recalled to France in 1870 during the Franco-Prussian War. He became a general of division in November 1870 and was made commander-in-chief of the Army of the North on December 3, 1870.

[14] The agrégation is a civil service examination in France for the highest level teaching qualification. It is usually only open to those who have studied four years at university.

[15] Maupassant is probably alluding to the growing predominance of the school of the Naturalists, centred around Émile Zola. Maupassant was once grouped with the Naturalists, but had since tried to distance himself from them (and any school). The Naturalists were actually a school of realist writers and artists, rather than being concerned in any especial way with nature.

[16] La forêt de Roumare is a French National forest and wildlife reservation of 4,000 hectares, west of Rouen. Jumièges is a village 25 km west of Rouen in the Seine-Maritime département (no. 76). Jumièges is famed for its Norman abbey that dates back to 1067 and was consecrated in the presence of William the Conqueror (1027-87, Duke of Normandy from 1035 and king of England from 1066).

[17] André Chenier (1762-94), French poet born in Istanbul; Alphonse de Lamartine (1790-1869), French poet and politician; Victor Hugo (1802-85), French poet, novelist and playwright; Alfred de Musset (1810-57), French playwright and poet.

[18] In French, 'ingénieur des Ponts et Chaussées', lit. 'an engineer of the Bridges and Roads'. The Corps des ponts et chaussées, a state body dealing with travel infrastructure and civil engineering, was established in 1716.

[19] The Ministère des Travaux Publics was a position in the cabinet of the French government from 1830-70, before it was largely subsumed by the Minister of Transportation.

[20] The Conseil Général is a regional assembly of a département.

[21] Sahurs is a village on the river Seine, directly opposite La Bouille (see n. 3 above), and is situated on the edge of la forêt de Roumare; the château du Bec is fictional.

[22] A seigneur was a title of feudal authority.

[23] Antoine Eugène Alfred Chanzy (1823-83), French general and governor of Algeria (1873-9). Chanzy commanded the XVI corps of the Army of the Loire who had the greatest French successes during the Franco-Prussian War.

[24] To characterize the German pronunciation, Maupassant often writes *f* for *v*, *b* for *p*, and *p* for *b* when the sergeant speaks, e.g., *fous* for *vous*.

Fragment Two

[1] The following list of possible character names and portrait of Doctor Paturel Jr are on a separate loose unnumbered sheet in the manuscript.

[2] Voltaire (pseud. François-Marie Arouet, 1694-1778), French writer; Napoleon Bonaparte (1769-1821), French emperor (1804-14, 1815).

[3] Microbes were still a relatively recent discovery, the word *microbe* being coined by Charles-Emmanuel Sedillot (1804-83) in 1878.

Fragment Three

[1] The discussion between Doctor Paturel Jr and Abbé Marvaux in the presence of the young cripple, André, is written on five pages numbered 1-5 in the manuscript. Page no. 3 appeared in facsimile in the Conard edition.

[2] The Académie royale de Médecine (known as Académie impériale de Médecine from 1850) was established in 1820 with its heritage stemming from the Académie Royale de Chirurgie founded by Louis XV in 1731, and was to answer to the government on all matters of public health. Nowadays it is called the Académie Nationale de Médecine and is based on the rue Bonaparte, Paris.

[3] In the French 'nom d'un chien', a euphemism for the exclamatory *nom de Dieu*.

[4] The Faculté de Médecine formed part of the Université impériale de France, in Paris, and was created in 1808, succeeding l'École de Médecine de Paris, it was reorganized in 1896 with four other Parisian faculties as part of the new Université de Paris.

⁵ Voltaire, *Le Sottisier* (Paris: Garnier, 1883), p. 164. Maupassant's 'L'Écriture prétend que Dieu a fait l'homme à son image, mais l'homme le lui a bien rendu' slightly misquotes Voltaire's 'Si Dieu nous a faits à son image, nous le lui avons bien rendu'.

Fragment Four

¹ The following passage is written on a separate unnumbered page in the manuscript and was the last of the five pages to be reproduced in facsimile in the Conard edition.

Auguste Dorchain's account of *The Angelus*

¹ Auguste Dorchain (1857-1930), French poet. Dorchain's account of the meeting and Maupassant's reading of *The Angelus* first appeared in *Les Annales politiques et littéraires*, XVIIIe année, 1er semestre, No. 884, June 3, 1900, and was then included in Albert Lumbroso, *Souvenirs sur Maupassant: sa dernière maladie, sa mort* (Rome: Bocca Frères, 1905), vol. I, pp. 62-5, which I have taken as my source.

² As Albert Lumbroso points out, 1891 should be read here—by August 1892 Maupassant had already been interned in a mental clinic.

³ Champel-les-Bains *or* Champel-sur-Arve is a wealthy neighbourhood in Geneva, where a hydrotherapy establishment was opened in 1873.

⁴ The river Arve is a tributary of the Rhône, flowing into it in Geneva.

⁵ Henri Cazalis (1840-1909), French physician and poet who wrote under the pseudonyms of Jean Lahor and Jean Caselli.

⁶ Properly called the Hôtel Beau-Séjour, a former mansion converted by the Swiss property developer and lawyer David Moriaud (1833-98). The hotel was bombed during World War II; the Hospitaux Universitaires de Genève now stand in its place. Maupassant was also staying in the Hôtel Beau-Séjour.

⁷ That is 1870-1, the year of the Franco-Prussian War. *L'Année terrible* (1872) is a collection of poems by Victor Hugo that take the Siege of Paris as their theme.

⁸ In the French, 'secouait la tête' which can mean either 'to shake the head (in saying no)' or 'to nod the head (in saying yes)'.

⁹ As Lumbroso correctly points out, Maupassant's suicide attempt took place in his Cannes apartment, not on board his yacht.

Hermine Lecomte du Noüy's account of *The Angelus*

¹ Hermine Lecomte du Noüy (1855-1915), one of Maupassant's mistresses. Her

account is from her book written with French author Henri Amic (1853-1929), *En regardant passer la Vie...* (Paris: Société d'Éditions Littéraires et Artistiques, Librairie Paul Ollendorff, 1903), pp. 50-62.

² Louis Ganderax (1855-1941), French journalist and critic and editor of the *Revue de Paris*.

³ Lecomte du Noüy here goes on to quote from *The Angelus* the interview between the Prussian commanding officer and the Countess de Brémontal which can be found translated herein on pp. 59-60.

⁴ Lecomte du Noüy here quotes from the discussion between Doctor Paturel and Abbé Marvaux which can be found herein on pp. 64-66.

⁵ Maupassant, *The Angelus*, Fragment III, p. 64 herein.

Mme de Maupassant's account of *The Angelus* to vicomte de Colleville

¹ The vicomte de Colleville's account is from the article 'L'oeuvre posthume de Guy de Maupassant' in *Le Figaro*, August 14, 1894.

Mme de Maupassant's account of *The Angelus* to Mademoiselle Ray and Dr Balestre

¹ Translated from Albert Lumbroso, *Souvenirs*, vol. I, 'L'Enfance et la jeunesse de Maupassant: Détails inédits racontés à Mademoiselle Ray et au Docteur Balestre par Madame Laure de Maupassant', pp. 338-9. Mlle Ray was the pseudonym of Renée d'Ulmès, a French writer; Dr Albert Balestre (1850-1922), chief doctor at the hôpital Saint-Roche, Nice.

² Probably in September, 1891.

³ Pauline Elisabeth Ottilie Luise zu Wied (1843-1916), the German-born Queen Elisabeth of Romania, the wife of King Carol I (1839-1914, r. 1881-1914), better known by her literary alias of Carmen Sylva under which she wrote poems, plays, novels and short stories as well as translations into German.

François Tassart's account of *The Angelus*

¹ Translated from François Tassart, *Souvenirs sur Guy de Maupassant par François son valet de chambre (1883-1893)*, ch. XVII, pp. 270-1.

² The Palais des Papes is a medieval Gothic palace in Avignon, overlooking the Rhône. It was the papal residence for much of the fourteenth century during the Avignon

Papacy (1309-77) when seven popes resided in Avignon in southern France before Gregory XI (c. 1336-78, pope from 1370) left the town for Italy in September 1376, returning the papal residence to Rome in 1377. The palace was built in two stages, with two distinct sections, the east and north-east wings being known as the Palais Vieux (Old Palace) and the west wing as the Palais Neuf (New Palace). Under instruction from Pope Benedict XII (d. 1342, pope from 1334), the Vieux Palais was built from 1335 by the French architect Pierre Poisson of Mirepoix in place of the old episcopal palace. Work continued during the reigns of popes Clement VI (1291-1352, pope from 1342), Innocent VI (d. 1362, pope from 1352) and Urban V (1310-70, pope from 1362), French architect Jean de Louvres *or* Loubière expanding the building with the addition of the Palais Neuf from 1345, the main courtyard, the Court d'Honneur, being completed during the reign of Urban V. Villeneuve-lès-Avignon is a town on the opposite bank of the Rhône to Avignon, in the Gard département (no. 30). In former times Villeneuve-lès-Avignon and Avignon were connected by the famous pont Saint-Bénezet (from the song 'Sur le pont d'Avignon'), which was built between 1171-85, and was over 900 m in length, spanning the Rhône. However the bridge suffered great flood damage in 1668 and since then further collapses mean that only four of the original twenty-two arches still stand today. In Maupassant's day Villeneuve-lès-Avignon and Avignon were connected by a suspension bridge that was built in 1846 by the French engineer Marc Séguin (1786-1875) and restored between 1886-9 by a fellow French engineer, Ferdinand Arnodin (1845-1924). This bridge was destroyed in 1940.

[3] The square is the place du Palais, bordering which is the Cathédrale Notre-Dame des Doms, a twelfth-century cathedral originally built in a Provençal Romanesque style. Becoming overshadowed by the neighbouring Palais des Papes, a cupola was added to Notre-Dame des Doms in the thirteenth century and later rebuilt in 1425. The cathedral is topped by a gold statue of the Virgin Mary that was added in the nineteenth century. The cathedral houses the Gothic tomb of Pope John XXII (1249-1334, pope from 1316) and Pope Benedict XII is also buried there.

[4] The reliquary of Saint Névia-Félicite is found in the Chapelle du Saint Esprit et de la Sainte Névia Félicité near the choir of Notre-Dame des Doms. Pope Pius IX (1792-1878, pope from 1846).

[5] Nîmes is the capital of the Gard département (no. 30) in southern France.

[6] Alexandre Dumas fils (1824-95), French novelist and dramatist.

www.ingramcontent.com/pod-product-compliance
Ingram Content Group UK Ltd.
Pitfield, Milton Keynes, MK11 3LW, UK
UKHW041451180426
11946UKWH00013B/149/J